The Alpha Who *Cursed* His Mate

Book Two of The Alpha Series.

Jazz Ford

Jazz Ford

ISBN: 978-0-6452231-5-6

DEDICATION

....

I dedicate this book to my dear friend Andie for all her love, support and encouragement. A beautiful friendship I'll always cherish.

CHAPTER 1

'Come on, Magnus, please play hide and seek with me,'
Nina begs me with her large, brown, doe-like eyes.

I walk towards her with abrupt haste. She steps back
until she feels the bluestone wall against her back. I tower
over her with ease. My mother, Astrid, the Luna of
Shadow Crest, always reminds me that when I was born, I
was double the size of a regular wolf baby and almost a
foot taller and much broader than any other ten-year-old.
She says I may even become the mightiest Alpha of all one
day.

Glaring down into Nina's eyes, I huff, 'I'm still mad at
you for tricking me into putting salt on my cereal this
morning instead of sugar,'

Nina's face lights up with a smile. 'The look on your face
when you ate it, though, was so worth it,' she giggles.

1

'Why do you always enjoy making me the laughingstock of the family? Do you hate me that much?'

'It's not like that, Magnus. You're my best friend, always and forever. We are just having fun,'

'Fun! You're not the one who gets into trouble for your little pranks and silly games. No one will take me seriously when I become the Alpha,'

'Of course, everyone will take you seriously, Magnus. You're overthinking it. Look, I'm sorry about this morning. Please play hide and seek with me?' She says, batting her eyelids at me.

I'm struggling to say no and instead sigh, 'Fine,'

'Yay!' She grabs my hand and pulls me along towards the large walled dam. 'Now, last time was boring though, so this time I brought this.' Nina removes a blindfold from her pocket and waves it like a flag in front of my face.

'A blindfold?'

'Yes, I'll blindfold you, and you count to a hundred because I know you have been peeking, and that's how you find me so easily.'

She isn't lying. I never fully close my eyes to see which direction she goes. Because she is so tiny and petite compared to me, I kneel so she can tie the blindfold around my eyes.

Holding my hand, she guides me to a nearby area. 'Okay, you can start counting now,' she lets out a mischievous giggle.

'Nina, this better not be another prank,' I yell out as she runs away, but she doesn't reply. Sighing, I start to count. As soon as I reach twenty, I feel a stronger vibration with each second. Following my gut instincts, I remove the blindfold to see I'm standing in the empty creek that leads water from the dam down to the river. I'm roughly fifty meters from the dam's gate. Warriors open the gate to release water from the dam when it's close to overflowing, which is right now. Water rushes down the creek, washing me away in the rapids. Nina runs alongside the stream giggling as I'm flung around in the water.

'Nina!' I yell and spit water out that has entered my mouth.

'Enjoying your bath?' She yells.

I grab a branch and pull myself out of the creek

'Nina!'

'Oh, don't be so mad, Magnus. You looked like you were having fun,' she giggles. Then, she turns and runs towards the Shadow Crest packhouse as soon as she sees me stomping towards her with a furious look on my face.

'I will get you back one of these days, Nina!' I yell and chase after her. Nina beats me back to the packhouse with great speed. She has always been very swift in her movements and is known to be the fastest runner in our pack, and can even outrun the warriors.

Entering the packhouse, I am met with my very unimpressed mother.

'Magnus! You are wet and muddy. What on Earth have you been up to?' She growls.

'It was Nina's fault,' I say, pointing at her as she sits like a proper lady at the table, looking oblivious to my words.

My mother stares at Nina, then back at me with a frown. 'Nina is as fresh as a daisy, as usual, Magnus. You are going to be Alpha one day. You need to take responsibility

4

for yourself. Now I suggest you go upstairs and have a proper bath,'

'But...'

'No buts Magnus, now!' Astrid points to the staircase, and I glare at Nina. She is trying to contain a laugh behind her hand.

Storming upstairs, I run a bath and struggle to remove the clothes clinging to my body and slip over. I lay there staring out the window at the overcast grey sky.

'Damn you, Nina, I wish if the Moon Goddess herself would curse you and not give you your wolf on your eighteenth birthday and remove your mate bond until the day I fall in love,' I say out loud.

A flash of lightning suddenly hits the roof of the packhouse, and thunder roars in the sky. I stand up in surprise at the timing of the thunder and lightning, wondering if it was a sign from the Moon Goddess. Nah.

I sit in the bath of bubbles and think of all the times I played with Nina. Chasing her across a field, she quickly leaps as I fall into a deep hole. Nina had, of course, led me to fall into the hole. I think about last year when it was my tenth birthday, and she pushed my face into my cake as I went to blow out the candles. Everyone, especially her, thought it was hilarious. Me, not so much.

Just like the time she put the itchy powder in my clothes. I spent half the day scratching myself silly and tearing my clothes throughout the day in agony. The entire pack laughed. I always felt humiliated, as if I was the family's joke. How am I supposed to be the future Alpha when no one takes me seriously because of Nina?

Maybe if I completely ignore her and keep my distance, my family won't see me as a joke anymore? I need my family to know I will take my role seriously as Alpha, and the only way to do that is without Nina in my life.

Content with my plan, I dry, dress, and join the packhouse downstairs for dinner. First, my Dad Alpha Ryker sits at the head of the table, and then it's my Mother next to him, but I have never seen her sit in her chair. Instead, she sits on my Dad's lap, and he wouldn't have it any other way. Next to my Mother's vacant seat is my brother Flint, then my sister Josie, the youngest. Being the next Alpha in line, I sit next to dad on the other side of the table. Then we have my Dad's beta, Seth with his wife Mia and their son Zak. Lastly, at the other end is Leon, who is in charge of the pack warriors and his wife Amelia with their two daughters, May and Nina.

Ignoring Nina, I smile at May, who blushes, and then I acknowledge my brother, sister, and the others. We eat our meals in silence, but Flint and Josie snigger and elbow each other.

'Care to share with the table what seems to be so funny?' Ryker asks them.

'We were just talking about how Magnus went for a swim today and got washed away and that it's probably the cleanest he has ever been,' Josie says and bursts into laughter along with Zak and May. I slam my fork down and cross my arms. I want to glare at Nina but remind myself to never look at her ever again.

'Kids, that is enough. Eat your dinner, or you can go without food. Your choice,' Astrid says with a firm voice. As we quietly eat our meals, my Dad talks about Vanessa and Alice, who fled from Shady Crest when I was born.

7

'The emerald pack caught sight of two female rogues and a young boy rogue in their territory and are certain the females were Vanessa and Alice. They followed them to another pack that is not on record and thought it may be a bunch of rogues creating their official pack,'

'Shall I send warriors after them, Alpha Ryker?' Leon asks.

'It's been ten years since they fled, and they haven't seemed to have caused any more trouble. Ten years on the run is already quite the punishment,'

'Well, if they are further south and keeping to themselves, I don't see the need to pursue them,' Astrid says.

Dad kisses her hand and nods in agreement.

CHAPTER 2

The next day I walk past Nina and ask May if she wants to climb some trees with Zak and me. I can see Nina's eyebrows crease in confusion out the corner of my eyes as May and I have rarely spoken to each other, nor have we ever played together.

'Sure,' she smiles.

'Okay, let's go,' I say and wave for her to follow.

Nina stands there watching us, then runs after us, 'Hey, I want to climb trees too, you know!'

I stop and face her, 'No, only my friends can join,'

'What are you talking about, Magnus? I'm your best friend?'

'You were never my friend,' I growl and regroup with others.

Nina's face turns sombre, with a hint of confusion.

'That's harsh, don't you think, Magnus? You and Nina have been the best of friends since you were both babies,' Flint says.

'No, our parents forced us to be friends, our mother's planning constant playdates every day, and if she were my best friend, she wouldn't be getting me into trouble every day. Nina no longer exists to me,' I argue.

Flint and Josie flinch and give each other a sad look.

'You are welcome to join us as well, just not Nina,' Flint and Josie hesitate at first but decide to follow us as May grabs my hand with a smile and drags me towards the trees, 'Come on, guys, let's see who can climb to the top first,' May giggles.

'Sorry,' Flint and Josie say to Nina, 'We want to go with them too.'

Nina looks down at her feet to hide the rogue tear sliding down her cheek.

We race towards the trees, and I'm the first to arrive with May. Moments later, Flint, Josie, and Zak arrive.

I could sense Nina watching us play from a distance, but I completely ignored her. Gripping onto branches one after another, I'm the first to reach the top of the tree. May climbs the same tree and sits next to me on the top branch.

Flint, Josie, and Zak shuffle along the vast, thick tree branches and make themselves comfortable as we all admire the view of Shadow Crest.

'We're so lucky to live here,' Josie says.

I couldn't agree with her more. A forest of trees surrounds Shadow Crest, with mountains in the distance. The buildings and houses are Victorian-style, with steeply pitched roofs, painted iron railings, and large porches. I look over at the Packhouse mansion. Excitement fills me for the day I become Alpha, but I can't help but feel something is missing. It's digging at my heart and soul, eating me away inside. I've never had this feeling before.

'Are you okay, Magnus?' May asks. I look to May, who is only two years younger than Nina, and, unlike Nina's Brown doe-like eyes, May's are blue. The rest of her features are like Nina's, except May's hair is much shorter.

'Yeah, I'm fine. Why do you ask?'

'Well, you seemed to be lost in thought and look sad,'

'Oh, sorry, I was just thinking about… things,'

'I know we have spoken little before today, but if you ever want to talk about anything, you can always… talk to me,' she says, hopeful.

'Thanks, May. I'm sure I will open up my thoughts to you one day,' I smile.

May blushes and casually looks away.

'Last one down is a rotten egg!' Zak yells.

We all quickly swing down and drop from one branch to the next.

'I won,' I smirk.

'You only won because Nina isn't here. We all know she is the fastest of us,' Josie pouts.

'If you mention her name to me again, Josie, then you can join Nina and become non-existent to me, too.'

Josie has a hurt look on her face and steps back while Flint glares at me.

'Let's go to Shadow Lake for a swim before we go back to the Packhouse,' May suggests.

I nod in approval and head towards the lake. With May by my side, Josie approaches and walks by my other side.

We arrive at the Lake. I pull my shirt off, then my socks and shoes, and dive into the cool water. Zak and Flint join me in the deep end while May and Josie roll up the legs of their pants and stay in the shallow area.

We duck under the water and hold our breaths for as long as possible. Zak is the first to swim back up for air, followed by Flint. Then, feeling like I was not enjoying myself as much as I usually would, I decided to swim away from them and hide behind a large boulder in the lake. I pull myself up for air and peek over the top of the boulder, watching Zak and Flint waiting for me to swim back up.

Their faces change to that of worry as they think I'm still down there.

'Magnus?' Flint says.

They all look at each other and nod. Then, holding their breaths, they duck back down while I stay behind the boulder for a few moments. I look over at May and Josie, oblivious to my joke. Flint swims back to the surface for air

13

and looks around in circles, confused about where I could be. Then Zak swims to the surface and panics.

'Magnus!' They yell, grabbing May and Josie's attention.

'We can't find him. You don't think he drowned, do you?' Flint asks.

They all panic—May and Josie cry.

Nina sprints out from the bushes and dives into the lake with great speed

'Magnus,' she screams each time she comes up for breath, frantic, tears pooling in her eyes.

I can't contain my laughter any longer. I lift myself onto the boulder in hysterics.

'Magnus! That was not funny,' Flint yells.

'Not cool, Magnus,' Zak growls.

'Come on, guys, don't be like that,'

I swim to the shore to where May and Josie are. As soon as I step onto the grass, I cannot help but sense someone behind me. I see tiny little Nina glaring up at me with her hands on her hips and tears streaming down her cheeks.

'Don't be like that? Are you serious, Magnus? We thought you had drowned. I thought you had drowned, and all you can say is, don't be like that? I thought you were dead,' she says, hitting my chest repeatedly.

That strange feeling consumes me again, eating at my inner conscience and soul. I look over at Zak and Flint, who are making their way out of the lake.

'We better get back home before mum sends the warriors out looking for us,' I say, treating Nina as if she was a ghost.

Everyone looks at her with sympathy. I don't know why. No one ever looked at me that way when she had played her stupid pranks on me.

We walk back to the Packhouse while Nina follows us slowly in the distance behind us.

As soon as we arrive at the Packhouse, I freshen myself up and join my parents for dinner with the rest of the Packhouse. Nina sits in her usual seat and tries to make eye contact. I pay her no attention and watch her shoulders drop out of the corner of my eyes.

'Bed early tonight, kids, the weekend is over, and you have school tomorrow,' Astrid says.

We all moan and grizzle except for Nina, who stays silent.

15

'Is everything okay, sweetie?' Leon asks Nina.

She shrugs and stays silent as she pushes the food on her plate around with her fork.

'What did you get up to today?' Amelia asks.

She looks up at me for a moment, but I keep myself busy eating my dinner.

'I climbed trees and swam at the lake with the others, Mum,'

'Sounds like you had a fun time,'

'Yeah, fun...' She mumbles.

CHAPTER 3

After a couple of months, Nina stopped greeting me each day, knowing I would not respond. Now in high school, she had become a loner. Keeping to herself in class and went to the library at recess and lunch.

May would elbow me and glare if she caught me staring at Nina, but she would always get jealous and cranky at any girl I glanced at.

'Stop elbowing me, May,' I growl.

'Stop staring at Nina then. You haven't spoken to her in seven years, yet you always stare at her. Besides, you should just be focusing your attention on me. Everyone knows we will be mates,' she beams.

'Not if I can help it,'

'Your such an ass Magnus,' she growls

'Yes, I'm told daily by many girls I have a nice ass,' I smirk.

'Who is telling you that? I demand to know their names right now,' she says, glaring at every female in the classroom.

'May, you need to get over it,'

'No, you need to get over Nina!'

I glare at May, making her cower back in her seat.

'I can't get over someone I was never into in the first place,' I snap.

May crosses her arms and looks away. We spend the last ten minutes of maths in silence. As soon as the bell rings, she clings to my arm as if we never argued, smiling as we make our way to the cafeteria.

I sit at the popular table that me and my friends sit at. Zak and Flint join me at my table, and our school friends, Paul and Claire.

Biting into my salad roll, I watch as Nina walks in and takes her seat in the far corner. Meanwhile, nearly every female is trying to grab my attention.

Claire places her hand on my shoulder and sits next to me.

'Hey, Magnus,'

'Hi, Claire,' I say and continue to eat my roll.

'So, I'm having a party on Saturday and wanted to invite you along,'

'Okay,' I mumble.

'Great! I was also hoping you would come to the party as, um, my date?' she says nervously.

I stare at her in thought. She is one of the most beautiful girls at school. She has lovely long legs, a decent-sized bust, long red hair, and green eyes. Thinking of how gorgeous she was, I stared back at Nina again. With her long brown hair, stunning brown eyes, and petite figure, I could easily wrap my arms around and lift her with one hand. But I can't help but wonder what her hair smells like? Does her skin feel as smooth as it looks?

Wait, why am I thinking of Nina this way? I cut her out of my life years ago for a reason, so why am I so curious about her? Now that I think about it, I don't think I've ever gone a day without thinking of her.

19

'Um, excuse me, Claire, you can't just ask him out when he is already claimed,' May growls.

'Magnus is a free man, May. You two aren't dating, and just because you think you are his mate doesn't mean you will be.'

Zak and Flint back away from the table just in time as May leaps towards Claire. A fight breaks out between them, and I sigh in disbelief.

Everyone in the Cafeteria crowd around them and chants, 'Fight, fight, fight!'

Nina rushes towards the crowd and sees Claire winning the fight. I go to pull them apart, but Nina jumps in front of May to protect her.

'Nina, what are you doing?' May yells as she touches the deep scratch across her cheek.

'Stopping you from getting seriously injured,'

'I don't need a freak like you to protect me,' she yells.

The cafeteria suddenly goes quiet, and all eyes are on Nina. I see deep sadness for a moment that she quickly hides.

'Claire is beating you with ease, and no one else seems to care,' she says, then looks at me.

I look away, avoiding eye contact.

'Yeah, well, I bet I could beat you with ease,' May yells, as she lunges towards Nina. I grab May around the waist and pull her back into my chest before she could harm Nina.

'That's enough, all of you,' I fiercely growl for everyone to hear. Everyone in the cafeteria submits and lowers their heads. 'May, go to the nurse's office and have your wounds cleaned up.'

May smiles and looks at me as if she has fallen in love. Of course, I care about May, but not how she wants me to. Right now, I want her out of here and away from Nina before she tries to hurt her again.

'Everyone, get back to lunch!' I yell. Everyone returns to their tables except for Nina, who stands there staring at me. As I sit down, she takes a few steps toward me.

'I know you don't want to hear my voice or even look at me, but I just wanted to thank you for stopping her. As much as she hates me, she is still my sister, and I could never fight or hurt her.'

My eyes, against my will, instantly connect with hers. Her innocent eyes remind me of a fawn that is about to be devoured by a wolf. My eyes trail down her smooth skin, her small nose, and to her lips. I wonder how sweet her lips would taste?

'Magnus?' Claire says. I shake my head of my thoughts. I need to stop thinking about Nina and move on if I'm going to be the best Alpha that everyone will respect and admire. Stepping closer to Claire, I ignore Nina and caress the red mark on Claire's cheek.

'Are you okay?' I ask Claire.

Nina's shoulders slump, and she walks away.

'I'm fine. May only slapped me once,'

I watch Nina's back as she continues to walk away. Maybe if I date Claire, I'll stop thinking about her?

'Claire?'

'Yes, Magnus?'

'I didn't have time to answer your question,' I smile.

Zak, Paul, and Flint watch on in anticipation.

'I would love to be your date for the party,'

Everyone in the cafeteria stops what they are doing and stares at Claire and me in shock. Disappointment and heartbreak etch into the faces of all the females.

'Seriously. You'll be my date?'

I nod my head. She jumps up and wraps her arms around me, squealing with delight. I gently place her back down.

Zak, Flint, and I finish our lunch and run some laps around the oval. Finally, the bell goes, and it's time for science class.

As we walk through the corridor to science, I am met with a furious May.

'Magnus! Why am I hearing that you are going to Claire's dumb party as her date?'

'Because I accepted her offer,' I say, then step around her to continue to class.

May runs back in front of me and places her hand on my chest. I look down at her hand, then back at her with a scowl.

'Magnus, you can't do this to me, to us. We should be together. I have always had feelings for you, and I know it's because we will be mates. If you go on this date with Claire, you would be practically cheating,' she sobs.

'It's not cheating, and I highly doubt we will be mates, May,'

'You don't know that we won't be mates!'

'Well, you don't know we will be mates. Only the Moon Goddess knows,'

A hurt look crosses her face.

'Please, Magnus, you can't ditch me for Claire. My reputation will be destroyed,'

'Is that all you care about, May, your reputation? How people view you? You should spend that time with people that care about you and want to be around you. It should never matter what anyone else thinks of you.' I growl and storm off into science class, running late because of May. I walk inside the room, and a strange feeling runs through my body as I see the only vacant seat is next to Nina.

CHAPTER 4

'Magnus, nice of you to join the class. Just because you
are the future Alpha does not mean you get special
privileges. Now take your seat before you get yourself
detention,'

I growl under my breath, 'Yes, Mr Thomson,' and plonk
my books onto the table and sit next to Nina.

Nina stiffens in surprise as I sit beside her. She looks at
me and is trying to contain a smile. I try to tune her
presence out and tune into Mr Thompson. He talks about
different types of soil that are low in nutrients and high in
nutrients. Nina's pen flicks back and forth as she listens to
Mr Thomson. Her hands are small and dainty, and her
nails have been freshly manicured and painted with a very
light, subtle pink. Her long brown hair drapes down her

arms. I watch as she tucks her hair behind her ear, revealing a gold earring and exposing her nape. My eyes focus on the nape of her neck. I feel my heart racing. I break out into a sweat and feel my heartbeat pounding erratically through my chest.

'Magnus... Magnus!' Mr Thomson yells. I fall off my chair. Everyone is laughing. I glare at the class, and they fall silent. 'For the second time Magnus. Take. Your. Seat,'

Nina gives me a look, but I grab my chair and take my seat, continuing to ignore her.

'As I said, the student you are all sitting next to will be your lab partners for the rest of the term,'

'What!' I say, slamming my fist on the table. It breaks in half. My books fall with Nina's, and all eyes are on me.

'I'm not partnering with Nina for the rest of the term!'

Nina raises her hand. 'Mr. Thomson, I have to agree with Magnus. I'd rather be lab partners with the classroom guinea pig in the cage. At least its I.Q would be higher than Magnus's,' she says.

The room roars with laughter.

'Quiet, quiet everyone,' Mr Thomson shouts, and the room becomes quiet minus the low giggles everyone tries to hold in. 'Now, Magnus, you have detention for being late, not paying attention, and destroying school property.'

'But...' I try to argue back. Nina laughs, and I glare at her.

'As for you, Nina, you will be lab partners with Magnus whether or not you like it, and you will also join him in detention today after school!'

'What! Mr Thomson, that's not fair,'

'As is life, Nina,' he growls.

Nina and I sit back in our seats with our arms crossed and backs facing each other since we no longer have a table to use, and we are both struggling to hold our tongues to not get into further trouble.

The bell goes, and everyone leaves as Nina and I squat down to collect our books. Of Course, the books mixed up when they fell. As we gather our books, we go to grab the same book, and I end up holding her hand instead. We pause and look at our hands. Her hand feels so soft and warm. We stare at each other for a split second, and I quickly let go of her hand as if it burnt me. Grabbing my last two books, I storm off to my last class for the day.

May and Claire have already arrived in English before me. They sit on the opposite side of the room, thank goodness. The only problem now is that they both pat the seat next to them for me to sit beside them.

Flint and Zak snicker in the back, wondering who I will choose to sit next to. Since I'm going on a date with Claire, I should probably get to know her better than I do, and it will help take my mind off Nina and what had just transpired in class with her.

May frowns as I take my seat next to Claire, and I see Zak pouts as he hands five dollars over to Flint. They had placed a bet as to who I chose.

Claire clings to my arm the same way May would.

'I can't wait until the party this Saturday,'

'Yeah, um, me neither,'

'So, what do you plan on wearing?' she asks.

'Er, clothes…?'

'Of course, you will wear clothes, dummy. What style of clothes?'

'a shirt and jeans, I guess.'

'You know what? I'm free after school tomorrow. Maybe I could come over and help you pick something out?'

I feel hesitant about having her over at my place. Do I even want her over? But then, my mind flashes back to the touch of Nina's hand, and I realise one of my many questions has been answered. Yes, her skin is just as smooth as it looks.

'So, what do you say, Magnus?'

'Huh?'

'About me coming over after school tomorrow unless you want me to come over today. I can cancel my shopping spree at the mall in the city with my girlfriends.'

'Can't today. I have detention after school with Nina,'

The pencil in her hand snaps in half, 'Detention, and with Nina?'

'Yup, I know. It's like the Moon Goddess wants to punish me. I do not know why, though.'

'Well, I feel for you, Boo-boo. It would be a curse to spend time with that freak. I will come over tomorrow after school then,'

I shuttered when she called me Boo-boo and felt anger build up when referring to Nina as a freak. I shouldn't care. Why do I care? I was angry when May called her a freak earlier in the cafeteria.

Claire caresses her fingers across my lower arm as we listen to Mrs Lofts discussing our upcoming essay assignment. Claire's caresses are making me cringe. She may as well run her nails across the chalkboard, as it would give me the same effect. I take her hand and hold it, so she stops touching my arm. She grins and looks over at May, who is mentally throwing daggers at me. Her skin isn't as smooth and lacks the warmth I felt with Nina's. Her hands are pretty clammy.

'Now open your textbooks to page 139 and answer the questions in your notebooks.'

I've never been so happy with Mrs Lofts giving me work to do. Happily releasing Claire's hand, I grab my pen and write my answers. I purposely answer them slowly until the bell rings as an excuse not to have to hold her hand again.

The bell goes. I'm happy to run home and get away from everyone, especially May and Claire. Then I remember I have dreaded detention.

Returning to my locker, I pack my books on the shelf and take my school bag. Josie runs up to me with her backpack.

'Ready to go home, brother?' she smiles.

'Nope, I have detention… with Nina,'

'Magnus! This is your chance!' she squeals.

'Chance for what?'

'To get on your knees and beg the hottie for forgiveness for being such a dumbass all these years.'

'Josie! Not going to happen,'

'But why not? I never understood why you would cut your best friend off like that. You two were so close and did everything together.'

'You wouldn't understand, Josie. You're not the one who will be an Alpha one day. I need to be respected, not laughed at.'

'I'm your little sister, daughter of an Alpha which means my mate will probably be an Alpha from a different pack, so yeah, I get you to need to be respected just as I do as a potential Luna, but I do not know what that has to do with Nina?'

'Forget it, okay? I'm going to be late for detention. I'll see you at home for dinner.'

Flint walks up to us as I'm about to walk away. Josie wraps her arms around Flint and sobs into his chest. Just great. After everything else going on, now Josie is upset with me.

CHAPTER 5

Without greeting Mr Thomson, I enter the science room, place my bag on a table, and sit in silence, avoiding eye contact with Mr Thompson and Nina.

'Late again, Magnus,' he huffs with his hands-on hip.

I shrug my shoulders and look away. Nina is sitting four tables away. It's obvious she also isn't happy to be here.

'Well, if you two think you are both going to sit here in silence, then you have another thing coming,'

Nina and I turn our attention back to Mr Thomson.

'I have borrowed some tools and a spare tabletop from the woodwork room. You will both spend detention fixing the table you broke,'

'What! But I never broke it,' Nina protests.

'Do not care, Nina, now come and take this hammer,' he growls.

I abruptly step down from my chair and march to the teacher's desk, muttering and mumbling in dissatisfaction. Nina takes the nails and hammer, and I carry the tabletop. Nina kneels next to the broken table and assesses it closely. I kneel opposite her and place the tabletop down.

Mr Thomson walks towards the doorway, 'I will be back in thirty minutes. I expect the table to be fixed,'

'Yeah, yeah,' I say, waving him off.

Nina clears her throat. 'Take the legs off the broken table. Then we can nail them into the new tabletop.'

Without saying a word, I take hold of the legs and go to pull it off, but Nina interrupts me, tapping me on the shoulder with a screwdriver.

'Just unscrew them like a normal person. Otherwise, you will either bend the legs or break them like you did the table,'

Ignoring her suggestion, I pull the leg, ripping it off, but the leg is bent and crooked as she foretold would happen.

'Great one, Magnus, a broken table and a bent leg, just great,' she huffs.

'Well, you fix it if you think you can do better.'

'If you didn't break it in the first place, Magnus, I wouldn't have to fix it.'

Our hands are on our hips as we glare silently at each other.

'Unbelievable,' she says and kneels by the other leg and unscrews the good leg with the screwdriver, as I should have done.

As she unscrews the last nail, the metal leg falls towards her. I grab it just before it hits her head. She looks up in shock, but I'm unsure if it's because she was about to be hit across the head or because I caught the leg before it knocked her out. I take the leg over to the new tabletop and hold it. She is still silent; her mind plays over what just happened.

'Well, are you going to come to screw this in while I hold it or not?' I growl.

She shakes her head at her thoughts and kneels right beside me. Our legs touch and I want to smile, but I don't.

Her dainty hands twirl the screwdriver in circles until the four screws are in. I lean across her lap to grab the bent leg, our faces so close for a moment that I smell her sweet breath reminding me of candy. Her lips have a clear coat of lip-gloss, I guess the strawberry flavour. I try to bend the leg back in place, but I seem to make it worse. Nina lets out a giggle, then quickly places her hand over her mouth to hide her smile. Something flutters inside my stomach, thinking I just made her laugh like that. It's a pleasant feeling, unlike the one I have had for years that carries a sense of doom.

She finishes screwing the bent leg in, and we stand back to look at the table that is on a slant. I place a book on it, and we watch as it slides off and bursts into laughter.

'What do you think Mr Thompsons is going to say?' Nina sniggers.

'Eh, who cares? It was fun making it, but then again, I don't want another detention,' I say, picking up the fallen book and placing it under the foot of the bent leg. The table is now levelled out.

We burst into laughter again, and the fluttering I feel inside grows. Mr Thomson walks into the classroom. 'I hope the table is… finished,' he trails off, looking at the bent leg propped up on a book.

'Magnus and Nina, detention again next Wednesday.'

'But!' we both try to argue with him.

'I told you both to fix it, not mangle it more! Now go home before I decide to call your parents,' he yells.

Nina and I both gulp and run out the door together. Seeing as we both live at the Packhouse, we both walked towards home together in silence, but it was a pleasant silence though.

Walking along the grass, she sees a baby bird chirping near a tree and rushes over to it. I follow her and watch as she scoops it up.

'The poor thing has fallen from its nest,' she says as she stares up at the tall tree, 'I'm going to put it back in its nest,'

'You can't climb up there, Nina. This tree is taller than what I would climb,' the bird chirps in her hands. It's pretty cute to look at. I gently scratch its little head to reassure it. It relaxes and snuggles further into Nina's hand. I can feel our bodies radiating warmth and realise how close I'm standing to Nina. I take a step back, giving her space.

'Well, I can't leave it here, Magnus. So I'm going up there with or without your permission,' she says, grabbing onto the first branch.

'Fine, but I'm coming with you only because if something happens to you, I will get the blame for it.'

Nina laughs. 'You won't get the blame for my actions, Magnus,' she says, now on the third branch.

I climb below her in case she accidentally falls. I don't want her to get hurt.

'Uh, yeah, I will. I always get blamed for anything you pull,'

Her laugh echoed through the trees as she grabbed the tenth branch. It was like beautiful music to my ears.

'Don't be so absurd, Magnus. You think too highly of yourself. I get into plenty of trouble myself each day, although once upon a time we used to get into trouble together, and we had so much fun doing so,'

I laugh, 'Fun? Anything we did as a child was far from fun, from what I remember,'

'Well, you remember wrong,' she says.

I look down at the ground.

We must be at least forty branches high.

'Enlighten me then,'

'Okay, remember when the laundry overflowed with bubbles, and we would play hide and seek to find each other?'

'Yeah,'

'Well, Magnus, that was your idea to fill the washing machine up with bubble bath and turn it on, and if you remember, I took the blame for it.'

I forgot she had taken the blame for it. She had to mop it all up and went to bed without supper. I snuck into her room and gave her a sandwich that night.

'And then there was the night we wanted to watch the moon from the roof. We climbed through May's bedroom window, but when you tried to open it, it wouldn't budge. You used such force that the whole window fell out and crashed onto the pavers outside. You went and hid in May's wardrobe, and I took the blame,'

She is right. I remember now. My parents would have been so mad at me for wanting to climb onto the roof in the first place, let alone breaking a window in the process of it all. I had run straight to the wardrobe, hid inside, and watched through the crack as Nina decided not to hide and took the blame instead.

'Well, I got in so much trouble because I wanted to protect you. You were my best friend. So I thought it would be fun to play a couple of pranks on you in return for some fun so that we would be even. The next morning, I heard the warriors say they would need to release some water from the dam. You were refusing to have your bath the day before anyway, so I thought it would be funny to have you stand in the creek while the water washed over you. I knew you were twice the size of most kids, so the water would only reach your waist. Still, you acted so dramatically that day as if you were going to drown when you could have just stood up and watched it flow past you, and you never spoke to me again until now,' she says,

giving me a sad look for a moment before looking away.

CHAPTER 6

And then it happened. It all hits me at once, that dreaded feeling but tenfold. That feeling when a hole in the ground opens up and just swallows you whole. Guilt. What have I done? She didn't make the Pack think I was a joke. It wasn't her responsible for all the pranks. It was me all along.

'There's the nest,' she says, not realising the bombshell she just dropped on my head.

Nina hovers over the nest. I climb next to her as fast as I can. She stretches her hands out to put the baby bird back in its nest.

'Careful,' I say, cupping my hands under hers. Nina looks up at me for a moment, and we lower our hands, gently placing the bird back in its nest.

'There you go, little guy,' I say and give it another gentle pat on the head.

The sun is setting, and the moon is rising. It's a breathtaking sight. We sit next to each other and watch its beauty in silence, the comfortable silence. We lean back on our hands, and our pinkies touch, but neither of us moves our hand away. I want to apologise to her. As Josie suggested, I want to get on my knees and beg for forgiveness. Josie was right. I had been a complete dumbass.

'We should get back to the Packhouse. We will get into trouble for being late home,' she says.

Nodding, I climb down first. A third of the way, Nina slips and falls. My hand wraps around her waist as she screams past me, and I pull her into the safety of my chest. Nina's arms cling back around my waist as she shakes from the fright of falling. She looks up at me, and I gaze into her eyes. Slowly, our lips draw closer like a moth to a flame. As they are about to touch, the branch cracks from the weight of both of us and breaks. I wrap my arms around her and land on my back, taking the brunt of the fall.

'Magnus! Are you okay?'

A few sharp pains bolt through my body as I sit up. I scrunch my face. 'I'll be fine,' I say, clearly in pain.

'No, you're not fine. Let me help you,' Nina says, putting my arm over her shoulder. 'You should not have done that,'

'Done what?'

'Take the brunt of the fall so I didn't get hurt,'

'It was nothing,'

'Sure...'

We make it back to the Packhouse grounds. Leon and two of his warriors run towards us.

'What happened, Magnus? Are you okay?' he says, taking over from Nina, helping to carry my weight.

'I'll be fine. I just fell over, is all,'

Nina gives me a confused look but says nothing.

'Well, we have all been worried sick about you two,'

'Sorry, Dad,'

'It's okay, Sweetie. I'm glad you helped Magnus home. Go to the dinner table. We will be there in a minute.'

'I'd rather just rest my back in my room rather than sit at the dinner table, Leon,'

'Of course,'

'At least in a couple of months, when you get your wolf on your eighteenth, you will heal quickly,'

'That's true,' I smile, excited at the thought that I will soon have my first shift and get to meet my wolf. I'm extra excited because I have Alpha blood. My wolf will be pure black like my dad's. However, my mother is a descendant of the Moon Goddess, so she has a pure white wolf.

'But until then, you will heal at a normal human rate,'

'Yeah, I know. Can you please have the cook bring my dinner up, Leon?'

'Of course,'

Forty minutes later, there's a knock at my door.

'Come in,'

It's Nina holding a plate of food.

'I, um, wanted to come to check on you and thought I'd bring your dinner,'

'Thanks,' I say, taking the plate and cutlery.

'I also wanted to say thanks for catching me from the fall.' She stands in silence, waiting for my response. I want to apologise to her, but the only word that comes out is.

'Anytime,'

She frowns, 'Well, I guess I'll leave you to it then,' she says and walks out the door.

I'm such an idiot, "Anytime," That's all I could say to her. I munch my meal down while I mentally scold myself. Maybe at school tomorrow I can make things right. There is another knock at my door.

'Nina?' I say.

'No, it's me, Josie,'

She walks in and sits in the chair beside my bed.

'I heard you fell over and hurt yourself, but I didn't believe Leon when he said that. My big brother and future Alpha hurt from a minor fall? No way, so I'm here to ask what actually happened.'

'Josie… You were right about Nina. I've been a jerk and don't even know how to make it up to her. She will never forgive me.'

'O.M.G Magnus, Are you okay? You must have hit your head. It's a concussion, right? Maybe a fever?' She says, placing her hand on my forehead. I whack it away.

'No, Josie, I'm not sick and don't have a concussion. After detention with Nina, we spent some time together. We climbed a tree, talked, and I realised I had made a mistake cutting her off seven years ago. She slipped, and I caught her, then my branch broke. I purposely took the brunt of the fall so she didn't get hurt.'

Josie blinks rapidly, processing what I just told her. She grabs my shoulders and shakes me.

'Tell her you're sorry!' she says right in my face.

'I know, Josie, I tried too, but I struggled to say what I wanted. I'm going to make it up to her at school tomorrow,'

'Well, I should hope so, Magnus. It's the least you can do,'

'I know I owe it to her; do you think she will forgive me?'

'As long as you don't stuff it up with her again, I don't see why not,'

'Thank Josie,' I smile.

'Oh, Flint and I never mentioned you and Nina had detention either,' she says, pretending to zip her mouth.

'Thanks, I appreciate it,'

'Well, I hope you will be well enough to go to school tomorrow to make things right again with Nina,' she smiles.

'Me too, see you in the morning,' I smile and watch her leave the room.

Okay, so my checklist for tomorrow. Beg Nina for forgiveness and restore our friendship. Too easy. Trying to fall asleep, I tossed and turned all night and had a bad feeling about school tomorrow.

CHAPTER 7

Sitting up, I look at myself in the mirror. My hair is a ragged mess from tossing and turning, and I can see slight bags under my eyes. My back feels okay, just a little tender, but nothing that can stop me from going to school. I shower and dress in jeans, a tight-fitting black shirt showing my muscular physique, and my favourite pair of black sneakers. As I comb my hair, it flings back into the shabby style, giving me the ruggedly handsome look instead of the sleek, pretty boy look I usually go for. I take my seat at the table for breakfast.

'Magnus, darling, how is your back, dear?' Astrid asks.

'It's fine. It wasn't anything major, to begin with.'

'I'm glad to hear,' she smiles.

51

I see Nina at the other end of the table, talking to her parents while eating breakfast. Josie is constantly looking between Nina and me. It's time to go to school. Nina grabs her bag and races ahead of us. I want to catch up to her, but she is faster than me. We have an assembly this morning and make our way to the hall. I sit as close as I can to Nina. There are five students between us. Claire calls out to me, races over, and sits next to me.

'Boo-boo, I've been looking for you all morning,' she says, clings onto my arm, and leans on me as the assembly starts. I can't shake her off and cause a scene, so I sit there quietly.

Principal Conrad stands at the podium.

'Good morning students, I would, first, like to remind you all that your rubbish goes in the bin and not on the ground. You should all know better by now. Second, I would like to welcome a new student joining our school today. I'm sure you will all make Moss feel very welcome.'

The school claps as Moss makes his way to the podium. He is almost as handsome as I am and has brown hair, but unlike my blue eyes, his are brown. You can tell he trains regularly. Although Moss isn't as big as I am, he isn't far off. I can't help but glare at him and decide I already dislike him.

'Thank you, Principal Conrad. I look forward to meeting you all and feel welcomed already,' he smiles. Everyone claps except me; I watch as he walks away from the podium with his smug face. Finally, after ten more minutes of Principal Conrad talking, the assembly ends.

Nina stares at Claire, still clinging to my arm as we leave the hall.

'We have the first class together, Boo-boo. Let's go,' she smiles.

'Great...,' I say, lacking any enthusiasm.

Nina sits in her usual spot and avoids eye contact, completely ignoring Claire and me. Then things become even worse. Moss walks in with a big grin showing his sparkly white perfect teeth. I almost want to throw up looking at him. His smile pissed me off, and I secretly hoped I could one day knock that smug smile from his face with maybe a couple of teeth out along with it. He stares around the room at the vacant seats, and his face lights up even more like a sparkler on a birthday cake when he sees Nina sitting in the far corner with no one near her. He sits beside her and puts his hand out to shake hers.

'Hey, I'm Moss. What's a pretty girl like yourself doing alone in the corner here?'

Nina blushes and shakes his hand.

'Oh, I'm Nina. I prefer to sit alone,' she says.

'Oh, would you like me to move? I didn't mean to intrude in your space?' he says sincerely.

'Actually, some company might be nice for a change, and you're new here anyway, so please make yourself comfortable,' she smiles.

They chatted quietly and giggled together throughout class. The bell finally goes, and I'm happy they will part ways.

'What subject do you have next? She asks him.

'Visual Art,'

'Me too,' she says happily, 'Let's go together then.' She smiles.

My heart sinks along with my gut. I've got English, so I'm stuck with Claire again, but at least Zak and Flint are in English. I try to think of who I know who has Visual Art.

'I'll meet you in English, Claire. I just got to stop by the men's room,'

'Okay, Boo-boo, don't take too long now,' she says, giving me a wink and blowing me a kiss. I try to hold the shudder as my body screams to release it. I rush down the corridor and find Paul before entering Visual Art class.

'Hey, Paul,'

'Yo-Yo, what's up, Magnus?'

'Um, not much. I have a favour to ask,'

'Oh, ok,'

'The new guy. I don't know what it is about him, but I can just sense something isn't right. Can you monitor Nina? I want to monitor her welfare around him. Being the future Alpha and all, it will be my duty to keep my pack safe, so why not now?'

'Sure, Magnus, I'll monitor both of them.'

'Great, and Paul, don't mention this to anyone, okay? It's just between you and me. Got it?'

'Got it,' he nods.

I run back to English and sit in my seat between Claire and Zak, with Flint beside Zak. We have to write an essay; I struggle to concentrate. Instead, I think of Moss and Nina.

'Everything okay, Boo-boo?' Claire asks.

Zak and Flint snigger at the nickname she gave me. I elbow Zak hard enough he flies into Flint. It shuts them up from laughing at me.

'Yup, fine, just struggling to concentrate is all.'

'Oh, my Boo-boo, do you have a headache? I can finish the essay for you?'

'Um yeah, it's a headache… sure,' I say, sliding my essay to her.'

I put my hand up.

'Yes, Magnus?'

'Um, I need to go to the men's room,'

'Okay, but be quick,'

'Okay, Mrs Lofts,'

'Oh, Boo-boo, you had just been to the men's room. Is it the runs?' she asks in front of the entire class.

I welcomed the hole that opened up and swallowed me whole yesterday to reappear and swallow me again.

'No, I don't have the runs, just be quiet, Claire,' I growl and storm out of the room, heading straight to Visual Arts class. I duck down outside the window and peek in. Moss is leaning over Nina, helping her with her work. He sits back next to her and pushes her hair behind her ear. I let out a loud growl, and everyone turns their attention to the growling window. I duck down just in time and crawl away furiously. Claire smiles when she sees me return to class, but she frowns when she sees the anger across my face.

'What's wrong, Boo-boo?'

'Nothing,' I growl.

'Well, if it's nothing, why do you sound so grumpy and angry then?'

'I'm not grumpy or angry.' I take a subtle deep breath to calm myself down and think of Nina's brown-doe-like eyes. 'I didn't sleep well last night, but now I know why.'

CHAPTER 8

It's lunchtime. I race to the cafeteria to ask Nina to sit with us for lunch, losing Claire along the way. As I enter the cafeteria, all eyes are on me from my loud, eager entrance. My eyes dart to the corner to see Moss sitting at Nina's table, having a good laugh. I barge back out of the cafeteria, passing Josie, Zak, Flint, and Paul. Claire manages to catch up with me.

'Where are you going, Boo-boo?'

'Anywhere but here,' I growl.

'What's his problem?' Flint asks.

They enter the cafeteria, and Josie can see why Magnus is upset. The new guy is hanging out with Nina and flirting with her. She frowns at the thought of it all, feeling sorry for Magnus.

Not wanting to be in the Cafeteria, I decide to hang out in the library for the first time in my life. I sit myself down at a table with the school nerds. They all gasp and stare at me while I bang my head on the table.

'Stupid, stupid, stupid, I'm so stupid,' I say.

'Um, Y-you're putting a dint in the t-table,' I hear from a squeaky nervous voice.

I look at her as she pushes her oversized glasses closer to her eyes.

'Pipe down, Pipsqueak. Can't you see I'm in the middle of a crisis?'

'Oh…-sorry, maybe talk about your p-problems and maybe we can h-help you with some advice?'

Giving her a strange look, I frown.

'Advice from a bunch of nerds. Are you crazy?'

'If I were c-crazy, I would have to have some kind of psychological d-disorder such as Munchausen or not be in touch with reality?'

'Okay, okay, I get it. Since I do not know what to do now other than bash my head against a table, I will tell you my problem, but none of you is to breathe a word of this to anyone.'

'O-okay,'

'So, I had a best friend as a child. I couldn't even ask the Moon Goddess for a better friend. One day seven years ago, I cut her off because I thought she was making my Pack not take me seriously and worry about me for when I become Alpha.

So yesterday, I realised that I'm an idiot and that it was myself making me look like a court jester. I decided last night I would beg Nina for forgiveness and repair our friendship today at school. But the school brought in a new student this morning, who you all saw, Moss. He has been glued to Nina's hip and flirting with her all-damn day. So that's my problem,'

'O-okay, I see. Doesn't Nina live at the Packhouse with you? You could always apologize at home,'

'Yeah, but this morning I felt like she was purposely not wanting to talk to me. Instead, she spoke to her parents more than usual and didn't glance my way.'

'Okay, is there a subject you have with her?'

'Yes, science and Mr Thompson made us lab partners,'

'P-perfect, that's when you can apologise,' she smiles.

'Thanks, I have science with her tomorrow,' I say, standing up to leave. 'What was your name, anyway?' I ask her.

'Pippa,'

'Thanks, Pip-Squeak, see you around,' I wave goodbye.

The lunch bell goes, and I complete my last two classes, happy to be going home.

'Oh, Boo-boo, I'm so excited to be coming to your house,' Claire says, taking my arm in hers.

'What are you talking about, Claire?'

'Boo-boo, don't tell me you forgot already? I'm coming over to help pick you out something to wear for the party on the weekend, remember?'

My stomach churned. I had utterly forgotten that Claire was my date for the party, and she was coming over. I'm lost in thought, trying to think of a way out of it, but I can't think of a decent excuse.

'Come on then,' she says, pulling me along to catch up with Flint and Josie.

'Hey Claire, aren't you going home?' Josie asks.

'No, Magnus invited me over. I'm going to help him pick out something to wear to my party. I am his date, after all,' she says.

Josie goes to glare at me but quickly smiles when Claire looks at her again.

'You are coming to the party too, are you not?' she asks.

'I guess I'll be there,'

'Great!' she says, squeezing Josie.

Nina walks behind us home. Every time I turn to see if she is still behind us, she stares at the ground. I can't see her face or emotion. She completely ignores me, and I'm not too fond of it.

We arrived at the Packhouse. My parents greeted us. They look down at Claire's hand, holding mine and frown.

'And who is this… lady?' mum asks.

'Oh, this is Claire, a… friend from school,'

'Oh, don't be so shy around your parents, Magnus. I'm his date for the party this weekend,' she beams.

'How... lovely,' Astrid says, forcing a smile. 'Well, you must come in then,' she gestures for us to enter. Claire and I go straight upstairs to my room.

'Wow, this room is so large, and you even have a bathroom. Please don't tell me that is a walk-in wardrobe over there?' Claire asks. She is so excited I'm waiting for her head to pop and blow streamers out everywhere like a party popper.

'Yeah, it's no big deal.'

'No big deal? This party is a huge deal, Magnus!' she says, entering the wardrobe. Instead of following her, I make myself comfortable and lay on my bed, hoping she will get bored and go home.

Instead, she comes out with a pair of black jeans, a belt with a silver wolf's head as the buckle, and five coloured shirts.

'You must try this one on first, Boo-boo,' she smiles and hands me a silver-grey shirt,'

'Can't you just pick one? Then I don't have to try it on?'

'This will be more fun, Magnus.'

Rolling my eyes, I sit up on the bed and remove my shirt.

'Magnus, my-my, you're so much more masculine than I even imagined,'

'You've imagined me shirtless?' I ask, feeling awkward.

Claire crawls up the bed and sits on my lap, pinning me.

'Oh, Boo-boo, I've imagined you with far less clothing on, she says' and smashes her lips to mine just as Josie enters with Nina.

'Magnus!' Josie yells.

In the utter shock and disgust of Claire kissing me, I push her away while I hear Josie angrily yell my name.

Nina and I make eye contact, and I can see the hurt in her eyes. She runs off down the corridor without saying a word.

'What the hell Magnus?' Josie says.

'Oh, sorry about that, Josie,' Claire giggles. 'I get how gross it can look when your brother is making out with his girlfriend. Next time we will try to be more discreet,'

'Discreet, are you serious?' Josie yells, then lets out a frustrated 'Grr,' and slams my door shut, leaving Claire and me alone.

CHAPTER 9

'What the hell Claire?'

'What's wrong, Boo-boo?' she says and tries to cup my face. I lean back, avoiding her touch.

'You can't just kiss me like that.'

'Why not?'

'Because you just can't.'

'Oh, I see, too soon?'

'Yes, too soon, Claire. We haven't even been on a date yet,'

'I'm sorry, Boo-boo, I'll hold off until then,'

'I'd appreciate that,'

'Now, are you going to try this shirt on?'

I take the shirt and put it on.

'Oh, very smooth, now try this one on.'

'This one is fine, Claire. We have an outfit picked there. It's time I take you home,'

'So soon?'

'Yeah, I forgot I have an um… assignment.'

'Oh, okay then,'

On my way out of the Packhouse, I run into Seth.

'Hey Magnus, where are you off to?'

'Taking Claire home. She lives near the school.'

'I'm about to drive past the school. I can drop Claire home if you like?'

'Oh, could you?' I say, a little too excited, to Claire's dismay.

'Sure,'

'Great!' I take Claire's hand and help her in the car and shut the door before she can kiss me on the cheek goodbye,' I had never been so happy to see the back of Seth's car driving away into the distance. I run back inside, and halfway up the staircase, I'm stopped by Josie storming angrily towards me.

'What is wrong with you? You said you wanted to make things right with Nina. Minutes later, you are making out with Claire!'

'Look, it wasn't what it looked like, I swear.'

Josie laughs. 'Are you serious? It wasn't what it looked like?'

'Yes, Claire gave me shirts to try on for the stupid party. As soon as I took my shirt off, she climbed onto me and kissed me as you walked in. I swear I didn't know she was going to do that. She caught me off guard.'

Josie takes a moment, calming herself down.

'You need to fix this, Magnus. You need to make things right with Nina, and after what just conspired between you and Claire. Well, let's just say it's going to take more than grovelling and apologies to fix this,'

'I know Josie, I'm going to see Nina now,' I say and walk around her, continuing up the stairs.

'Nina?' I say gently, knocking on her door. 'Nina?'

The door opens abruptly. Nina holds the door open with one hand, and her other hand is on her hip. Her face shows no emotion.

'What do you want, Magnus?' she says, sending a hot shiver down my spine, saying my name.

'I wanted to come to apologise to you?'

'For what exactly?'

'For what you just saw between Claire and me.'

'Why are you apologising for something that's not my business?'

I'm stunned by what Nina is saying. She left and ran down the corridor. I thought it upset her seeing me with Claire?

'You ran off upset when you saw us, I thought?'

'You thought wrong. Why would I be upset? We have meant nothing to each other for seven years, so why would I care now?' Her words hit me like a knife in my heart. Her words were brutal, but I could see where she was coming from. 'What you do isn't my business and hasn't been for seven years, so why would I care whose mouth you put your tongue down? Now, if you excuse me, I'm going to bed. Goodnight, Magnus,' and slams her door in my face.

Leaning our backs against either side of the door, we slide down and stare at our feet with sadness, although she won't admit it. I know I hurt her again. She will be in the Science class tomorrow. That will be my opportunity to speak to her. I return to my room, step into the shower, and bang my head against the wall in frustration. Once I've finished sulking in the water, I climb into bed for another restless night of little sleep.

The morning arrives, and I sit at the table for breakfast to find Nina completely ignoring me again. She runs to school ahead of us again.

On arrival at the school, I walk to my locker with Josie and Flint on either side of me. I look over at Nina. Moss has an arm above Nina, leaning into the locker. She blushes and giggles as he whispers in her ear.

Josie and Flint observe them and then give each other a worried look.

'Let's get to class,' Flint says.

'What do we have first?'

'Physical Ed, let's get our training gear on,'

PE is just what I needed to help me burn some of this frustration out. We go to the change room, change into shorts and tank shirts, and walk to the oval where Mr Tilley waits to train.

While we wait for the rest of the class, I begin stretches with Flint and a few other guys.

'You got to be kidding me?' Flint says, looking over my shoulder. I look to see what his problem is, only to repeat Flint's words.

'You have got to be kidding me?'

'Hey guys,' Moss smiles and waves and stretches with us.

'What are you doing here?' I snap.

'I have PE,' he smiles. 'I'm Moss,' he says, putting his hand out to shake mine. Instead, I stop stretching, cross my arms, and glare at him.

'Ok, fellas, let's begin with a few laps around the oval, and you start now,' Mr Tilley says and blows his whistle. I jog past Moss knocking into his shoulder, and he immediately realises I don't like him. Moss races to catch up to me. He jogs by my side with a smug grin that keeps growing. If that smug smile gets any bigger, he'd be the joker's doppelgänger. Flint and I increase our speed to lose him, but he keeps up with us. He whacks his shoulder, nudging me with force. I do the same back. Then the next thing you know, we are both on the ground tackling each other. He punches me in the jaw. I hit him in the left eye, and he punches me in the right eye. I hit his cheekbone. Mr Tilley runs toward us, blowing his whistle. 'Stop! Stop right now, break it up!' He continues to yell at us, but neither of us listens to him. I grab Moss's arm, turn him onto his stomach, wrap my other arm around his neck, and keep him in a lock hold, cutting off his airway. He is about to pass out before using his free arm to grab my precious jewels and twist them.

'Argh,' I yell and sit back, releasing him whilst I cling onto my goods.

He turns around, and we glare at each other, panting. We both have black eyes, bloody noses, and bruises on different areas of our faces.

'Magnus, what has gotten into you? And Moss, you are new here. You should know better about getting into fights. Now both of you see the school nurse and report to the principal's office.'

'Yes, Mr Tilley,' Moss and me grizzle.

Mr Tilley sends Flint with us to make sure Moss and I didn't get into another fight along the way. We walk through the corridors, and it horrifies students at the sight of us as we walk past the windows. Nina sees from her class and races out with a gasp. I smile and feel warm as she races out to check on me. My mouth drops open when she races up to Moss and wraps her dainty little arms around him. I can hear my growl across half the school grounds. Nina steps back from Moss.

'What happened to you?' she asks, staring at me, then at Moss.

'I was in PE training, and that guy was unfriendly and tried to knock me over when we were running laps. We ended up in a fight. I've never met the guy before, so I don't know what his problem is,' he says, glaring at me.

Nina marches up towards me in anger. 'How dare you! How dare you get into a fight with Moss like that! Just because he is my friend and treats me with kindness, unlike someone else, I know Magnus! Does not give you the right to destroy another friendship!' She storms back to Moss; she takes a handkerchief from her pocket and gently dabs the blood away from his face. He cups his hand over hers and gives her a sweet, brief peck on the tip of her nose.

'Thank you, Nina.' he says, smiling down at her.

My blood is boiling. I felt so angry that I could spontaneously combust and take half the school buildings with me. Flint places his hand on my shoulder.

'Best to just see the nurse. Standing here watching is only going to make matters worse.'

I march past them in anger and stomp into the Nurse's station.

'Magnus, what on Earth happened to you?' Nurse Carla asks.

'Got into a fight.'

'Well. Who with?'

'The new guy, Moss,'

'Where is he? Did he sustain any injuries?'

'Probably a few extra bruises than I, but he already has someone attending to him.'

'Take a seat.'

I took the seat while Nurse Carla cleaned my face up as best as possible.

CHAPTER 10

'Do you want me to call your parents to come to pick you up from school?'

'No, I'll stay,'

'I'd prefer you go home and put ice on your face, Magnus.'

'Look, I'm staying, okay? If it makes you feel better, I'll rest here for the next period until recess.'

'Okay, I'll get you an ice pack then.'

She returns a moment later and hands me the icepack; I hold it against my swollen black eye for the next hour. Then, finally, the recess bell goes. I toss the icepack onto Nurse Carla's table and walk to the cafeteria. Students stare and whisper as I walk by them.

'I heard he knocked Moss out and almost killed him.'

'Well, I heard he picked Moss up with one hand and threw him halfway across the oval,'

Well, at least the whispers and rumours were to my liking. Entering the cafeteria, Claire lets out a gasp and races toward me. She cups my face.

'Boo-boo, I heard there were rumours a fight broke out. I did not know it involved you. Oh, my poor snookums,' she says, embracing me. I notice Nina and Moss watching Claire smother me with concern and worry. My face lowered closer to hers, and I pecked her on the lips without even thinking about my action. Nina looks away, but Moss's steely glare intensifies.

'Oh Boo-boo,' Claire blushes. I place my arm over her shoulder and pull her close to my side. Josie brings a tray of lunch over for me.

'I heard you got into a fight with Moss. You know Mum and Dad will flip beans when they see your face, right?'

'Yeah, I know, but that's the least of my problems,' I say, glancing at Nina. My fist slams down onto the table as I see Nina and Moss kissing. Everyone at the table jumps.

'Boo-boo, what's wrong?'

Josie gives me a sympathetic, knowing look.

'They forgot to put the cheese in my roll,' I lie.

'Oh, here have mine then,' she offers and swaps them over. She has been so infatuated with me that she even ordered the same lunch as me. May joins us, angrily plonks her food tray down in front of us, and bites into her ham roll as if she was biting the head off a small critter. She glares at Claire and chews loudly.

'Gee, everyone is such a grump today,' Paul says with a nervous laugh.

We sit there in silence for the rest of lunch. The bell goes, and I realise I have Science with Nina now. Moss walks her to science and gives her a long kiss that involves eating her face. He smiles at me and leaves to go to his next class.

Nina placed her books on the mangled table we had made together. I sit next to her, but we both sit silently, refusing to speak.

'Okay, today you will fill out this questionnaire with your lab partner. If you don't know the answers, it will tell you what page you can read to find the answer in your

textbooks. You have forty-five minutes.' Mr Thomson
says.

He places a questionnaire sheet on each table. Five
minutes go by, and neither of us has moved.

'The questionnaire isn't going to fill itself out, Nina and
Magnus. So get to work, or I will fail you both in science.'

We grumble and mutter under our breaths and take our
pens to fill it out. We both go to take the sheet
simultaneously but grab each other's hands instead. I
don't want to let go, but Nina pulls her hand away in a
flash. We both take the end of the paper. She glares at me.

'Let go. I'll fill it out,'

'Let me at least fill a couple of questions out,' I say.

The sheet of paper tears in half and Mr Thomson walks
over and slams the sticky tape down.

'Again, you broke it, you fix it, then fill it out,' he growls.

I hold the two strips of paper without speaking while
Nina tapes them together.

'I'll fill out the first half, and you do the rest,' she snaps.

'Fine,' I say and cross my arms.

Once she has answered eight questions, she angrily slides the sheet toward me. I pause and gaze at her.

'What happened to us, Nina? We were getting along so well the other day, we almost, well, you know? and now we are worse than ever?'

'The other day should never have happened. Besides, Moss asked me to be his girlfriend today, and I said yes.'

'You only just met him; how could you go out with someone you don't know. What if he is an axe-wielding maniac or has bad intentions for you?'

'Why do you care, Magnus? You have never cared for me. So I think it's obvious to both of us that you are jealous,'

'Jealous?' I laugh.

'Yes, you are jealous of Moss and feel threatened by him. Otherwise, you would not have taunted him into a fight. However, I highly doubt he is dangerous. If anything, he has been charming, loving, and caring towards me. You should focus on your girlfriend and return to your old ways of pretending I don't exist,'

'I don't want it to be like this,'

'Magnus, you are the one who made it like this. So now you get to live with it.'

Sadness consumes me. I take the questionnaire, fill the rest out slowly, and hold back my tears.

Mr Thomson collects our sheets as the bell rings

As I walk to English, I see Sean, the well-known school bully who has cornered Pipsqueak. He is harassing her. He flicks her glasses off your face.

'Now empty your pockets,' he growls in her face. Scared, she does as she is told and empties her pockets of any coins.

I grab Sean's neck and hold him two feet off the floor against the wall.

'Got a problem with my friend here?' I snarl in his face.

'Oh, sorry, I didn't know she was your friend,' he says nervously.

Whilst holding him up, I look at Pipsqueak shaking.

'How often has he been taking your money?' I ask her.

'E-everyday,' she replies in her squeaky little voice. I turn my attention back to Sean.

'Empty your pockets,' I tell him.

'What?'

'You heard me, empty your pockets, or I'll make your face look as pretty as mine,' I say. Sean looks over my bruised and banged-up face and quickly empties his pockets.

Releasing my grip, he falls to the ground.

'If you ever go near Pipsqueak or any of her friends again, you will face my wrath,'

Sean scrambles to his feet and bolts down the corridor.

'The money is yours. Take it,' I say to Pipsqueak and continue to class.

'W-wait,' she says, running up to me.

'What?'

'T-thank-you for s-stopping him, Magnus,'

'No worries, Pipsqueak,' I say, walking away. I notice Nina is standing with Josie waiting for their class door to be unlocked. They had both witnessed me protect one of the school nerds.

'It's P-Pippa… by the way.' Her words cheerily echo down the corridor behind me.

CHAPTER 11

It's the end of the school day. Josie and Flint meet at my locker.

'Hey, bro, ready to go home?' Flint asks.

'I'd rather them not see my face, but I don't have a choice. So I suppose we better get home so I can face the music,'

As expected, Nina was home before us, and mum and dad were standing at the front door looking as mad as hatters.

'Magnus, we received a phone call from the school today stating you got into a fight with the new boy and, from looking at your face, I'd say they gave us accurate information,' Mum says, unimpressed. Dad walks to me and places his hand on my shoulder.

'Son, what were you thinking? You will be Alpha before you know it, and here you are, beating up the new boy. You have some explaining to do,'

'I may have accidentally nudged him at PE, and it turned into a fight,'

'And why did you accidentally nudge him?'

Perfect timing. I look over Dad's shoulder as Nina approaches. Dad raises his eyebrow at Nina, then back at me.

'I see… well, I hope we don't have a repeat of this terrible situation, but I'm glad you are okay son,' he pulls me in for a hug and whispers in my ear.

'Next time, knee him good and hard in the balls, son. That girl is worth fighting for,' Shocked, I contain my tiny smirk and give dad a slight nod instead.

I remain in my room until it's time to join the Packhouse for dinner. Leon, Seth, Mia, and Amelia cringe at my face. Mum, of course, sits on dad's lap.

'Your father and I have been organising your wolf ceremony. We have invited five different packs,' she smiles.

'Why so many packs?'

'Well, since you will be eighteen and have your wolf, you will find your mate and become Alpha. However, just in case your mate isn't in this pack, I figured we would help you find her quicker by having as many unmated she-wolves present for the ceremony,'

'Mum, are you for real?'

'Yes, I'm for real. I'm so excited for you! When I met your father while working at the diner, I didn't even know wolves existed and didn't even know I was one. Your father entered the diner like he owned the place and kept talking about vanilla and cookies. Jim and I thought that was what he wanted to order, but it was my scent. It's funny now that I think about it. I fled from your father and tried to pull a runner when he said we were mates and had explained it to me,'

'You ran from dad when you found out he was your mate?'

'Yep,' Mum laughs.

'Your mother fled from me a few times, but before I knew it, she couldn't get enough of me,' Dad laughs.

'So true,' Mum giggles.

'What if the she-wolf I want isn't my mate? What if I want to choose my mate instead?'

Mum drops her fork, and the colour from her face fades. Everyone has stopped laughing and stares at me instead. Finally, mum seems to have come to her senses and stairs at me.

'Magnus, it's frowned upon for good reasons choosing a mate instead of accepting the mate the Goddess blessed you with.'

'But...'

'But, nothing,'

'Mum!'

'She is right, son. Choosing a mate instead of accepting the one the Goddess blessed you with can cause many problems, not just for you but your entire family,' Dad frowns.

'What if I don't like my mate?'

'Why don't you at least wait and find out who she is first?'

'It would be easier just to choose,' Mum abruptly stands from dad's lap.

'It's too dangerous, Magnus. Please wait and find out who she is first,'

'I don't see what the big deal in choosing is,'

Mum slams her hand on the table.

'Magnus, choosing a mate takes her away from her true mate. Is that fair to her? People die. People get hurt when you choose a mate. How do you think my mother died when I was a child and your grandfather and our entire pack of Mooncrest? Unless your mate has passed away and the she-wolf, you like, has also had her mate pass away, then it will not happen,' Mum storms from the room, leaving me in shock.

'I did not know that… I didn't mean to upset mum,' I say to dad.

'She will be okay. She has had a very rough past and wants the best for you kids,'

'Great, now you upset mum too,' Josie sighs and crosses her arms.

'Josie,' I scowl.

'Who else have you upset today?' Leon asks. The room goes silent. No one dares answer, not even Nina herself.

'I'm going to bed,' I say, standing up. I walk up the stairs and crash land on my bed.

The dreaded sun hits my face. I don't even remember falling asleep. I must have been exhausted. It's Saturday. I put my shorts and tank shirt on and spend the day at the Packhouse gym. I've got Claire's party tonight. Part of me wants to go, the other part doesn't, but everyone will expect me there. I shower and put the black jeans on with the silver-grey shirt and my belt with the silver wolf buckle. A lot of the swelling and bruising has gone down. There is a knock at the door. I open the door to see its mum.

'Mum, I've been meaning to talk to you. I did not know the effect choosing a mate could have. I'm so sorry, mum. I never meant to hurt you,'

She welcomes the hug and embraces me with a tight, loving squeeze. She is so tiny she can barely reach around me.

'I was coming to let you know Claire rang and is hoping you will arrive at her house soon to help her greet everyone,'

'Yeah, I guess I can go now, Mum,'

She smiles. 'You have a great night and no more fights, okay?'

'I'll try my best to behave, mum.' Waltzing downstairs, my breath is caught. Nina stands by the window near the front door, looking out. She has a red fitted dress that sits just above her knees with little black heels and a matching clutch purse. I want to tell her how beautiful she looks. I take a step toward her.

'Wow, Moss is a lucky man,' Flint says as he and Josie approach, Nina. Flint is wearing a white shirt tucked in suit pants, and May is wearing a black dress with straps. Flint sees my steel gaze on him and laughs nervously.

'I'm assuming Moss will be here to pick you up any minute?' Flint asks her.

'Yep, any minute,'

'What!?' I say.

Nina tilts her head to look at me.

91

'Moss is taking me out for dinner. Then we are going to Claire's party afterwards,' she smiles. I want to punch the front door, but I know I will knock it off its hinges and mum and dad would be angry. So instead, I walk out the front door and do not say a word.

Flint and Josie run outside after me.

'Aren't you going to get a lift from Seth with us?'

'No thanks, I'll walk. The fresh air will do me good.' I huff.

CHAPTER 12

Claire stands on her front lawn looking for me. She is wearing a pink fitted dress with one sleeve and some frills with her freshly curled hair draped over one shoulder. Claire looks simply gorgeous. She races up to me with a smile on her face.

'Oh Boo-boo, I'm so happy to see you,' she says, giving me a peck on the cheek. I realise I may have been ungrateful towards Claire all this time. She seems to like me a lot, and although she can be pretty overbearing, she has been nothing but supportive and sweet towards me. I can't help but feel Nina will never forgive me and never want to be my friend again. It's a hole inside me that will be there forever, but I shouldn't make others who care about me suffer. Nina has moved on, although I would have preferred her to move on with anyone other than Moss. I can't help but sense something is off about that guy, but I need to focus on what is in front of me.

'You look lovely, Claire,'

She steps back and does a twirl. 'I'm glad you like it. Let's go inside.' Her house is very tidy. She leads me to the kitchen to a vast island table. There are a few different platters she has prepared.

'Wow, this looks great, Claire,'

'Really?'

'Yeah, can I try one of these things?'

'Of course, you can. It's called a vol-au-vent, by the way. There are a few different flavours,'

I pick one up and take a bite. It tastes amazing.

'These are delicious,' I say, reaching for another. Claire takes my hand away from the food.

'Let's wait till everyone gets her,' she smiles.

'You know maybe you should consider becoming a chef?'

'I am hoping to open a restaurant one day.' She says, opening the fridge. She hands me bottles of soft drinks. I set them up on the table, walk to a cupboard, take a few stacks of cups, and place them near the drinks. Claire stands back and looks around with hands-on her hips. 'What am I missing?... Music, of course.' She runs into the loungeroom and turns on the stereo. 'Everyone will start arriving any minute,' she says, dancing towards me. The doorbell rings, and we answer the door greeting six guys and two girls from our school. Josie, Flint, Zak, and May turn up a few minutes later. I place my hand around Claire's waist. 'Hey, come in. Good to see you all.' Claire says. May glares at my hand on Claire's waist and stomps past us. Paul and a few others turn up with him and join the party. The house is full of teens dancing, chatting, and playing card games within twenty minutes.

I notice Paul following May around, trying to flirt with her.

'Let's dance, Boo-boo,'

'How bout we have a drink first, lemonade or cola?'

'Cola, please, Boo-boo,'

I pour her a cola and sit on the couch, patting the seat for her to sit next to me. She sips her cola, places it on the coffee table, and leans her head on my chest. I wonder where Moss has taken Nina for dinner. Are they laughing and enjoying each other's company? I notice Sean, the school's notorious bully, has joined the party.

'Ready to dance?' Claire asks. I was about to say no until Nina and Moss entered through the front door, giggling and laughing. Moss immediately wraps his arms around Nina and dances with her.

'Sure,' I stand up, pull her close, and keep both hands on her hips.

'This is so much fun!' Claire yells over the music.

I try to dance with Claire to keep as calm and relaxed as possible and show everyone I'm not fazed about Nina and Moss.

Claire wraps her arms around my neck and pulls my face closer to hers. We share a long kiss as Claire's hands move down to my chest. My mind keeps telling me to relax and enjoy the kiss. My shoulders relax, and one hand leaves her hip and slips behind her head, pulling her in for a more passionate kiss. The room fills with 'oohs' and wolf whistles at our show. Not wanting to dance anymore, I take her hand and go to the kitchen for the delicious food she made.

'This is the best food I've ever had,' I say, chowing a bit of everything down.

'Oh, Boo-boo, stop it, you are just saying that,' she blushes.

'No, I'm serious, Claire. You can cook for me anytime,' I smile.

Once half the platters are empty, she pulls me in for another long kiss. She gives me a seductive look and takes my hand, leading me up the staircase to her bedroom. Nina and Moss watch as we go up the stairs.

We spend half an hour making out on her bed, she goes to unzip her dress, but I grab her hand and stop her. She gives me a worried look.

'What's wrong, Boo-boo? I thought you wanted this? Don't you want me?'

'Claire, I want this, but I'm not ready for us to take that step yet,'

'Why not? Don't you find me attractive?'

'Of course, I find you attractive. It's just that I'll be eighteen in a few weeks, and I want to wait and see if you are my mate or not,'

Her bottom lip trembles, and her eyes well up.

'Are you saying you don't think I'll be your mate?'

'No, well, no one knows but the Moon Goddess. So let's wait a few more weeks until we take that step, okay?'

'Even if we aren't mates, we can still… you know, make love to each other,' she says, fluttering her eyes at me.

'I don't want to hurt you, Claire. I don't want to hurt more people than I already have, okay?'

'There is also the chance that I could be your mate so we can still be together in the meantime, right? Like boyfriend and girlfriend? Until we at least know?'

'Sure,' I say and kiss her forehead, 'We should go back and join the party?'

'They probably all think we have been doing the deed up here,' she giggles. She is probably right. Great, I've probably pissed more people off now.

We return downstairs. Claire has a big grin on her face. Everyone is staring at us, but most are being discreet about it. I sit on the couch, and Claire clings to my arm and sits next to me. The next thing we know, May comes stomping out from the kitchen with a bucket filled with ice cubes and water and throws it over us.

'You bitch,' Claire says as she is about to strike May across the face. I gently grab her wrist in time.

'Claire, she's upset for obvious reasons. I'll handle May, go upstairs and change,' I say as I watch Moss sneak out the front door alone.

'May, I know you have wanted to be with me. I know how it feels to not be with the person you want to be with,'

'No, you don't,'

'I'm telling you now, May, I do. I know you're hurting, but I am with Claire now. So be angry at me all you want but don't take it out on her,'

Josie runs up to me with a small towel.

'Are you okay?'

'Yeah, I'm fine, Josie. I'll be outside drying off.' I can't help but sense Moss is up to no good. I look around and

99

can see him jogging in the distance towards the trees. There is someone there waiting for him. I can make out the silhouette of the person. As I'm about to jog closer, I hear Nina in distress in the backyard.

CHAPTER 13

'I said no, now leave me alone!'

'Come on, babe. Just a little kiss is all I'm asking for,' Sean says.

'Let me go, you jerk!'

Sean is holding her arms against the wall of the house. She can't move. I walk up behind Sean and put him in a lock hold. I break his arm. Nina jumps at the sound of his arm snapping.

'If you ever touch her again, I will kill you,' I say as my eyes turn entirely black. There is a force inside me struggling not to kill him, not to rip his head off now. It's overwhelmingly powerful. I have felt nothing like it in my life. I'm fighting myself as I also fight Sean down as he tries to escape. He is screaming and holding his broken arm. I fling him into the swimming pool. It's that, or I snap his neck, and the last thing I need right now is to end up in wolf prison.

I hunch over, heaving. My muscles feel as if they are growing bigger. I think I'm slowly growing bigger and stronger. I'm overwhelmed with anger, and I'm struggling to control it.

Everyone has run out of the house into the backyard to see why Sean is screaming. Everyone steps back slowly in fear as I fight myself.

There is a voice in my head.

'Let me take over, let me kill him!' he snaps.

I cling onto my head, 'No stop, leave, go away,' Finally, I fall onto my knees and feel a bone in my back snap.

'He's shifting!' someone yells.

'He isn't eighteen yet. No one has shifted early before?' says another voice.

'Someone needs to go to the packhouse and get the Alpha and Luna straight away,' Paul yells. A few people run off together towards the packhouse as I continue to fight my wolf.

The pain I'm in is immense. I toss and turn on the ground. Another bone snaps.

'Shh, it's okay, Magnus, you're going to be okay,' I hear from the sweetest voice I've ever heard. Nina is approaching very slowly with caution. My inner wolf relaxes for a brief moment from the sound of her voice. But then, he tries to take over again.

'It's okay, try to relax. Fighting your wolf will only make it more painful,'

'How do you know that?' I managed to say with a strained voice.

My dad told me the pain is far worse during your first shift if you fight it.

'If I shift, my wolf might kill Sean,'

'I won't let your wolf kill him. The jerk has already peed his pants when he ran off screaming, holding his arm,'

I can't help but let out a small chuckle that Sean peed his pants. The pain subsides quite a bit, and I realise Nina has my head on her lap, stroking my arms that are growing fur. Completely relaxed and a few more bones snap, my face morphs into my wolf. My tongue sticks out, panting happily as Nina strokes her fingers through my fur.

Everyone is watching and gasps.

'He is a pure white Alpha. Alphas are black?' Zak says in amazement. I want to keep my eyes on Nina's face, but I look down at my paws to see fluffy white fur. They're right. My coat of fur is white.

'Magnus, this is amazing,' Nina says in awe. She studies my face closer and strokes her fingers down my back a few times. 'Tell me I'm dreaming?' she asks, looking at everyone.

Flint approaches and crouches down beside her.

'You're not dreaming, Nina. It's incredible, though, and I've never seen a wolf this big he is even bigger than dad's wolf,'

'Thank you, Magnus, for saving me back there. I was looking for Moss. He had vanished. I came outside to see if he was out here and instead found Sean, who, well, you saw the rest,' she says, trying not to sob. I step towards her and nudge her face, wiping the rogue tear away. She wraps her arms around me the best she can and cries.

'What's going on out here?' Moss asks, approaching the crowd. Everyone parts creating a path. He freezes over at the sight of not just me but Nina crying with her arms around me. I let out a deep horrifying growl that makes everyone cower. Nina looks up and sees Moss. I take a few steps towards Moss, baring my teeth and growling. He takes a few steps back, and I forward a few more.

'No, Magnus,' Nina says and crouches in front of me. 'You can't hurt him, Magnus,' I give her a look as if to say where was he when you needed him? She looks away in dismay as if she had read my mind.

'It doesn't matter now, Magnus. Regardless, Sean's actions are not Moss's fault.'

She was right, it wasn't his fault, but I couldn't help but feel he was up to no good anyway. My wolf tries to fight for complete control to kill him.

'Magnus!' My parents shout my name.

As soon as they approach, Moss takes the opportunity to take Nina's arm and pull her back. I let out a growl.

'Magnus, you've shifted?' Ryker says.

'And he is pure white like my wolf,' Astrid says, stunned.

'Have you ever seen a white male Alpha before?' Ryker asks Astrid.

'No, but like me, he is a direct descendant of the Moon Goddess. Perhaps my grandfather was a white wolf or a grandfather before him, or he could be the first pure white alpha wolf to exist? But either way, the Moon Goddess has bestowed this on him,' Astrid smiles, 'You are so beautiful, my son,' she says and hugs me.

'Can you shift back?' Dad asks. I don't want to shift back just yet. Instead, I look toward the trees and let out a loud howl.

'A run it is then,' Ryker says. My parents shift into their wolves. My wolf is at least six inches taller than my dad's. Everyone watches as all three of us howl in unison and run towards the woods, just as Claire comes out of her house after changing different dresses to see what is going on.

'Who's that wolf, and where's my Boo-boo gone too?' she asks, confused.

Zak approaches her and places his hand on her shoulder. 'You might want to sit down for this?'

Claire passes out to everyone's amusement after Zak catches her up to speed. The wind whips through my fur. My paws pound against the dirt, and my massive tongue hangs out, collecting the odd flying insect. I feel so free, so wild and powerful.

My parents are only meters behind me as we run with the wind. As we howl into the night sky, more wolves from our pack join us and howl in unison to celebrate the arrival of my wolf. Sitting on a mountain top, one by one, they line up and bow, exposing their neck, showing complete submission and loyalty. It's midnight. I run again through the woods before returning home to the Packhouse with my parents, Seth, Leon, Mia, and Amelia. They all shift into their human forms and wait for me to shift.

'Relax, son, close your eyes and imagine yourself in human form, and you will shift back. It won't hurt,'

Closing my eyes, I imagine myself in human form as pain sears throughout my body as I shift back. My howl of pain turns into a human scream.

CHAPTER 14

My mother falls to her knees and tries to comfort me. I'm covered in sweat and feel immense pain.

'What is wrong with him, Ryker?'

'I don't know. Magnus shouldn't be in pain. I've never seen a shift like this before. Something isn't right. Let's get Magnus to his room and call the Pack doctor,'

Seth, Leon, and my dad carry me to my room.

'He's got a fever,' Astrid says, touching my forehead.

Seth leaves to get the Pack doctor while my mother stays by my side, wiping my face with a cold face washer. My whole body is shaking, and I cannot speak.

'Maybe it has something to do with shifting early?' Ryker suggests.

'Maybe,' Astrid frowns.

The pack doctor arrives and takes my obs.

'He has a fever, but I'm struggling to see how it has anything to do with shifting. And you mentioned he was in immense pain when he shifted back?'

'Yes, he was screaming in pain, doctor,' Ryker says.

'I see. Well, I don't know what to say. I've never seen anything like this. I'll take some blood samples and see if I can find anything. But, for now, keep Magnus cool until his fever breaks,'

'Thank you, doctor,' Ryker says and shows him out the door.

The morning arrives, and I'm still shaking. Mum had fallen asleep at some point. Her head rests on my bed.

Someone knocks at my door, stirring her awake.

'I'll be right back, Magnus,' she whispers.

Opening my door, she greets May, Nina, Zak, and Flint.

'Dad just told us Magnus has a fever? Is he going to be, okay?' Josie asks.

'I'm sure once the fever breaks, he will be fine,' Astrid assures them.

'Can we see him?' Nina asks.

'Yes, I'm sure Magnus would like to see you all,'

They all step inside my room and approach my bed. Everyone can see I'm shivering and sweating. I'm mumbling, but it's incoherent.

'Shh, save your energy, just rest.' The sweet voice says.

I feel Nina take my hand and hold it between her two hands. She sits in the seat my mother spent the night in and holds my hand tighter. 'You go rest, Luna. I'll stay and watch over him for you.'

'Thank you, Nina,' Astrid smiles.

'You get better soon, brother,' Flint says.

'Yeah, we have school tomorrow and would rather you go with us,' Josie says.

They all leave the room except for Nina, who stays by my side, holding my hand.

'The whole town has been talking about your early shift last night and that your wolf is pure white. Even some of our neighbouring Packs have already heard. Some of the Alpha's want to come to see you for themselves to see if it's true.' She takes the face washer from my forehead and rinses it in cold water, and wipes the sweat from my face.

111

She walks over to the window and opens it wide, allowing the fresh breeze to whirl through my room.

Nina stays by my side for the next hour until my parents enter with the pack doctor.

'He still has the fever? There was nothing unusual about the blood results, which doesn't help explain why he shifted early and now has a fever. There must be more to it, like something we can't see?'

'Like magic?' Nina says, gaining everyone's attention.

Doctor Reed pauses in thought for a moment.

'Exactly like magic,' he says.

'I don't understand,' Astrid says

'I have a friend, Yiselda, who may be able to help. Her visit will have to remain a secret, though. No one must know she was here or that she exists?' He warns.

'Why is that, Doctor Reed?' Nina asks.

'Because Yiselda is a witch, and with your permission, I'd like her to come here to meet and assess Magnus. She will see if any magic is involved.'

'But I thought witches haven't existed in over a hundred years?' Ryker says.

'There is a small coven of witches that no one knows about that still exists. They don't make themselves known to the public for fear of being hunted and killed,'

'I see. If you think it will help Magnus, you have my approval,' Dad says. The doctor nods and takes his leave. Nina sits back in the chair and holds my hand until Claire comes running up the stairs.

'Boo-boo,' she yells, barging into my room.

'I heard what happened last night and was told you have a fever?' She says and discreetly nudges Nina to move. Nina frowns and stands with my parents. Claire takes the seat and grabs my hand, squeezing it too tight for my liking.

'Claire, I'm sure Magnus appreciates that you have come to see him, but he needs his rest, my dear,' Astrid says.

'Oh, Luna, don't fret. I will take over and watch over him while you all rest. It's the least I can do since I am his girlfriend,' she says while giving Nina a quick glare.

'You can stay with him for a couple of hours, Claire, and then I'll be back to watch over him,' Astrid says.

'Okay, Luna, I'll take good care of him,'

'I'm sure you will…,' Astrid frowns.

They take their leave, leaving me alone with Claire.

'Oh Boo-boo, let me freshen that face washer up for you,' she says, dipping into a bucket. She doesn't rinse the excess water and plops it onto my face. Water dribbles all over my face and pillow. I may as well be floating in the middle of the ocean at this rate. 'That breeze is messing my hair up, Boo-boo. Give me a moment while I shut the windows,'

I tried to tell her to leave the windows open, but no words left my lips. The room became stuffy within minutes, and my fever felt even worse.

'Oh Boo-boo, I'll hop in bed beside you.'

The last thing I needed was body warmth. I already felt sticky and slimy and overheated as it was. Nina lies beside me, sliding her fingers through my hair, and tugs at it as she tries to soothe me. It is annoying me, and I can't do anything about it. Finally, after almost two hours of intensive care from Claire, my mother and Nina entered my room.

'Magnus! What has happened? You look even worse!' Astrid gasps.

'Oh, I thought he was improving?' Claire says.

Nina, fetch the pack doctor for me and show Claire out along the way, please,'

'By Boo-boo, I'll come to visit you after school tomorrow,' she says, kissing my lips that I can't even move. They are dry and flaky from dehydration.

Nina happily shows Claire out of the packhouse and calls for the doctor. She returns to the room and opens the windows. She looks around the room and takes a spare pillow.

'Luna, could you lift his head while I swap the pillows over, please?' Astrid nods and lifts my head as they change the pillow over. The dry, fresh pillow feels much better, and the breeze from the window is refreshing.

'He needs water,' Nina says, filling a glass of water from the bathroom sink.

She sits beside me and lifts the glass to my lips. I take as many sips as I can. The doctor arrives with Yiselda. Nina stands up and moves away so Yiselda can assess me.

'Can you tell me what is wrong with my son?' Mum asks. Yiselda doesn't approach me. Instead, she looks over at Nina.

'He is reacting to a curse,' she says.

'A curse? What curse?' Astrid asks.

Yiselda points her finger at Nina

'Her curse.'

CHAPTER 15

'My curse?' Nina says.

'Yes, your curse,' Yiselda replies.

'Are you implying Nina has been playing with magic and cursed my son?' Astrid asks.

'No, but she has a curse shadowing her. It's affecting Magnus,'

'I'm sorry, but you must be mistaken? I'm not cursed,' Nina says.

Yiselda looks Nina up and down.

'Oh, you're cursed, sweetheart. I can see it lingering all around you,'

'What kind of curse? How do I get rid of it?'

'For what kind of curse, I do not know and how to break it. Only the one who cursed you knows how. Until then, you are stuck with it,'

'How do I find out who cursed me, then?'

'Only time will tell,' she looks over at Magnus and approaches.

She hovers a hand over him and says an incantation. 'The fever will break soon. But, in the meantime, until the curse breaks, I suggest you tell him to avoid shifting,'

'Why is that?' Astrid asks.

'It's going to hurt every time he shifts.' Yiselda takes her leave without saying another word.

'We need to have a pack meeting immediately,' Astrid says to Nina.

Everyone leaves the room—my fever breaks due to the spell Yiselda used. I can walk to the bathroom and decide to shower. I feel so much better afterwards. I find my favourite black tight-fitting shirt and dark-coloured jeans and put them on. As soon as I'm ready, I walk down the stairs to find a meeting is being held.

'Magnus, you are looking better,' Seth smiles.

'Yeah, I feel heaps better,'

'You better join us, son,' Ryker says.

Seth and Mia sit at the end of the table while Nina sits with Leon and Amelia on the left side of the table. I take my seat next to my father.

'As we all know, someone has placed a curse on Nina, but it's also affecting Magnus,' Ryker says.

'I don't understand who would want to curse my daughter,' Amelia cries. Leon rubs her back.

'We will sort this out, Honey. We will find out who cursed her and have them break the spell,'

'Nina, can you think of anyone who would want to curse you?'

She shrugs her shoulders and looks down with a sombre look.

'Everyone loves Nina, Mum. I don't understand who would curse her,' I say.

'Other than it is affecting Magnus, this curse hasn't seemed to have affected Nina. She looks and sounds like Nina; she is gifted with great speed and has good grades. So how is she cursed?' Leon says.

We are all at a loss and are silent in thought for a few minutes, trying to make sense of it all.

'There isn't much we can do other than monitor Nina and Magnus and figure out what the curse does and who is behind it. I also think we shouldn't tell anyone about it for Nina's safety,' Astrid says.

'Why wouldn't Nina be safe, Mum?'

'Magnus, you are the future Alpha of the pack. Some pack members will go to great lengths to protect you. Many would even kill to keep you safe,'

Nina and I give each other a concerned look and nod our heads in agreement. We part ways. I decide to go outside and sit on the staircase. Unexpectantly, Nina joins me and sits beside me.

'Magnus, I just wanted to say how sorry I am that I caused you to be unwell and that you won't be able to shift easily. I don't want to hurt you,'

'It's not your fault, Nina,'

She cries. I place an arm over her shoulder and pull her closer as she cries into my chest.

'But it is my fault. Someone cursed me, and it's hurting you,' she cries.

'It will be okay, Nina. We will figure this out,'

'Magnus?'

'Yeah?'

'Do you wish sometimes we could go back in time and do things differently?'

'Every day. I wish I wasn't stupid and didn't ignore you for seven years,'

'Do you mean that, Magnus?'

'Every word,'

'We can't go back in time and change the past, but we can change the future right now,'

'How so?'

'Let's forget the seven years never happened. Let's be best friends again,'

'Really? You mean that?' My stomach flutters and my heart is racing with happiness.

'Every word,' she smiles.

The next day we walk to school together.

'I'm glad you are well again,' Zak smiles.

'Thanks, me too,'

'I'm glad to see Nina is walking to school with us for a change,' Josie smiles.

121

'Me too,' I say again. Nina and I smile at each other.

We arrive at school. I have science with Nina first.

We walk in giggling and laughing and take our seats at our wonky table.

'Great to see you two laughing for a change instead of fighting,' Mr Thomson says.

We opened our textbook and completed our worksheet with no drama. The bell goes for the next class. Moss approaches Nina, wraps his arms around her, and lifts her up. She squeals with delight while he holds her up and gazes into his eyes before they kiss.

As hard as it is, I keep my cool. Moss puts her down gently.

'I'll see you later, Nina,' I say, waving goodbye. She waves back.

'I thought you hated him?' I hear Moss ask her.

'We have put our differences aside and are once again friends,'

'I see…,' he says in a deep voice. He glares at me, 'Let's get to class, babe, before we're late.' He says and leads her away.

Claire races towards me. 'I'm glad you're better. Let's get to English class,' she says, holding my arm.

Lunchtime came around quickly. Claire and I made our way to the cafeteria. Nina waves and smiles at me from her table with Moss by her side. I wave back.

'Why are you waving at Nina? Magnus?' Claire asks.

'Because she is my friend, Claire,'

'But I thought you weren't talking to each other anymore?'

'Well, we are now,' I say and munch on my food.

I chat with Flint, Zak, Paul, and Josie. May keeps quiet but glares at Claire the whole time.

The bell rings.

'What class do we have, Flint?'

'PE…'

Great, PE with Moss, way to ruin my day.

Flint, Paul, and I change into our shorts and tank shirts and hit the oval.

Moss keeps up with us, trying to intimidate me, but it doesn't work. We completely ignore him and finish the three laps.

'Right boys, time for some dodgeball,' Mr Tilley announces. 'I want you all to form two groups,'

We form two groups; Moss is on the opposite team.

Mr Tilley places his hand on my shoulder.

'This team will throw the balls first. After that, the other team must dodge the balls and not get hit,'

My team lines up, and we throw them at random members of the opposite team. Moss is the last one on the oval still playing. He has excellent stamina and agility but is not as good as me. I aim the ball carefully and throw the ball. It taps his chest.

'You're out, Moss,' I say with a smirk.

He glares.

'Right, swap sides now, boys,' Mr Tilley yells.

As we pass each other, Moss whacks my shoulder with his. I want to rip his head off, but I contain my anger and ignore him, making Moss even angrier.

He kept aiming for me and missing. He threw the ball with significant force, hoping to injure me. I'm the last player on the oval, and it's been over twenty minutes.

Mr Tilley blows his whistle.

'Time to pack up, and Magnus, well done.' He says.

I walk away with Flint, Zak, and Paul back towards the school building until I feel a sudden pain in my head, and everything goes black.

CHAPTER 16

I wake up in the nurse's office with a throbbing headache and look around the room.

Flint is with me.

'What happened?'

'Moss decided dodgeball wasn't over yet... he ran up behind you, threw the ball at your head with all his strength, and knocked you out. He is in the principal's office,'

Nina runs into the nurse station and takes my hand.

'I heard what happened. Moss should not have done that. I'm so sorry. I will talk to Moss and make sure he does nothing stupid again,'

'Nina, it's not your fault. You don't need to apologise,'

'He just doesn't like us being friends again, but he will have to accept it,'

Claire runs in and takes my hand from Nina's grip, 'Boo-boo, are you okay?'

'Yeah, every minute that goes by, the pain subsides,'

The nurse walks in, 'That's because you have your wolf now. You will heal quickly,' she smiles. 'Do you feel well enough to return to class?'

'Yes, I think I'll be fine,' I say and get up.

'Thanks for checking on me, Nina. I appreciate it,' I say, waving.

Claire glares at me for a moment. 'You know Boo-boo,' she says as we walk away, 'I think you're spending too much time with Nina. I'm feeling very neglected, you know,'

'I think you might be exaggerating, Claire. I only have science with her and wave to her when we cross paths at school. Although we both live in the Packhouse, we don't see each other often other than meal times, and even then, her seat is at the other end of the table. I have more subjects with you than I do, Nina,'

Claire perks up, 'Well, when you put it that way,' she smiles.

My wolf is restless and wants to go for a run. I want to shift and race through the woods, but I push it to the back of my mind, remembering the witch had advised me to avoid shifting.

I'm happy it's the end of the school day. Claire kisses me goodbye, and I catch up with Zak, Flint, Josie, May, and Nina.

'Wanna climb some trees?' I say.

'All of us?' Nina asks. I nod.

'Last one, there is a rotten egg,' Josie yells.

We all race through the woods on the way home to our favourite tree climbing spot near the lake. Nina is the first to arrive, then me, Flint, Josie, and Zak.

'Zak's the rotten egg,' Josie laughs.

We climbed the trees. Burning my excess energy was helping to keep my wolf at bay.

We reach the top and sit together, silently watching the village of Shadow Crest for a while.

The restlessness was returning. We climb halfway down the tree, and I take my shirt and pants off and jump from the branch into the deep lake. Droplets of water from the splash reach the others.

'Magnus!' They all laugh. Once they climbed down, they hopped into the lake.

'You boys have to turn around so you don't see us in our bra and knickers,' Josie yells. Zak, Flint, and I roll our eyes and face the other way in the water.

May, Josie, and Nina strip off their clothes. Josie yells out once they are shoulder-deep in the water.

'You can look now,'

We turn back around and splash the girls. They squeal and splash us back.

'Let's see who can hold their breath the longest, two at a time. The winner goes on,' Josie says.

Flint and Josie go first. Josie wins. It's Zak's turn to go against her.

This time, Zak wins and goes against May. Zak wins and goes against Nina, and Nina wins. It's my turn to go against her.

We both sink deep into the lake together on the count of three. We are a good two metres deep. We come closer to each other, trying not to laugh as we will lose air.

Suddenly, our eyes connect, and we relax in the water. My hand slowly reaches Nina's face. My thumb caresses her skin, and she turns her face closer to my hand, closing her eyes.

When she opens her eyes, I'm closer. I want to taste her lips. We inch closer and closer until our lips almost brush each other. Then, a sudden force pulls Nina up out of the water. Confused, I swim straight up after her.

May is pulling Nina's hair and trying to scratch her face.

'You know I like him. How could you?' May screams. 'It's bad enough I have to see him with that skank Claire, but you, Nina? And you always wonder why I never think of you as my sister!' She screams. Flint and Zak pull May away from Nina, who is now crying.

'Nothing happened, May,' Nina yells back.

'That's because I stopped you,' she storms out of the lake and grabs her clothes. I quickly pull Nina towards me, and she flinches.

'Are you okay?'

'No, I'm not okay,' she cries.

'We will take May home,' Zak says. Flint goes with him.

'Magnus, we can't do this. That was too close. We almost... and you're with Claire, and I'm with Moss. It isn't right,'

'I know, but... it feels right,'

'You will be Eighteen next week, Magnus, you already have your wolf, which means you can find your mate now, and in case you haven't noticed, we aren't mates as you would have felt the mate bond. I also assume Claire isn't your mate because the mate bond would keep you by her side,'

My heart sinks. I hadn't even thought about the mate bond. The warm tingle, the electricity that runs through your body when you touch each other, wasn't there. I had made eye contact with Nina and Claire, and my wolf never submerged and declared either of them as my mate. 'Claire will be hurt when you tell her she isn't your mate, but it will hurt her more if you stay with her and find your mate in the meantime,'

Again, she is right. I look down into her eyes for a moment. I try to memorise this moment. Her beautiful doe-like eyes always get my heart racing.

'Magnus, I'm sorry, we can be friends, but from a distance. I think it's better if we stay apart as much as possible for the sake of the future Luna, your mate, and to avoid us getting hurt. I'll be eighteen only a couple of months after you, and I'll have my wolf and be able to tell if Moss is not my mate, then I will have to end the relationship and pursue my fated mate, just like you have to do,'

She gives me an empathetic look before I can say anything, swims out of the lake away from me, and returns to the Packhouse. I stay in the lake, frozen in place, for what feels like an hour. As I leave the lake, I look at my pruned fingers and collect my clothing from the ground. I return to the Packhouse, now dry and dressed. Nina isn't anywhere to be seen.

'She is in her room, in case you are wondering?' Flint says.

'She said she wants to be left alone and will have dinner in her room tonight,' Josie frowns.

May comes storming her way across the hall towards me. As she opens her mouth to yell at me, I quickly speak first.

'May, can I talk to you privately for a moment?'

Her feet stop, and she gives me a look of confusion, which turns into a glimpse of hope.

'Yes, I think we are overdue for a private moment,' She smiles.

We go outside into the courtyard, away from prying eyes and ears.

'May, you should be the first to know that Nina nor Claire are my fated mate,'

'What? How'd you know that?'

'Remember, my wolf arrived early. I can sense my mate now,'

'Oh! But wait, that means I'm not your mate either, am I?'

'I'm sorry, May, I never meant to hurt you, and I never meant to hurt Nina, and now I have to break up with Claire tomorrow at school, who is also going to be hurt by it. Today in the lake, that was my fault, not Nina's, and it was unfair of you to attack her like that. Just as I owe you an apology, you also owe Nina one,'

She sighs and looks away, thinking about it.

'You're right. Jealousy got the better of me. Nina probably wishes I was dead. I've always been so nasty to her because I see how she looks at you all the time,'

'Nina loves you, May. She would never wish that upon you. She even tried to protect you against Claire that day you got into a fight,'

'You're right. I don't deserve Nina's forgiveness,'

I place my hand on her shoulder.

'Leave that for Nina to decide,'

May wipes the tears from her eyes.

'Thanks, Magnus.'

CHAPTER 17

I don't want to go to school today knowing I have to end
things with Claire. Sometimes I have to wonder if it's me
who has a curse. Everyone who seems to care for me ends
up hurt. I force my feet out of bed, knowing what I need to
do. I get dressed, wash my face in the basin, and head
downstairs for breakfast. Everyone is already halfway
through breakfast. I must have slept in. Everyone greets
me except for Nina. Her eyes stare vacantly at her bowl of
cereal as she swivels the milk around with her spoon, lost
in thought. As soon as I sit down, she stands up and grabs
her schoolbag to leave.

'In a hurry?' Leon asks her.

'I'm meeting up with Moss so we can walk to school together,'

'Okay, honey. You have a great day,'

'Thanks, I will, Dad.'

She runs out the door. Zak, May, and Josie are ready to leave. I grab my bag and join them.

'Have you talked to Nina yet?' I ask May.

'No, last night I went to her room, but she ignored me and wouldn't open the door,'

'Nina has gone through a lot. She needs some time, and then the opportunity to talk will arise,'

'I hope so,' she frowns.

We arrive at the school. I walk to my locker and hear my pet name being called out.

'Boo-boo, I missed you,' Claire smiles. She leans up to kiss me, but I take a step back.

'Claire, we need to talk,'

'What's the matter, Boo-boo?'

'There is something I need to tell you, and I'd prefer to tell you privately,'

'Whatever you have to say, you can say it here. I'm sure it's not that bad, whatever it is,'

'Claire... you know how I have my wolf now?'

'Yes,'

'Well, that means I can sense and feel my mate, and I don't feel the mate bond with you,'

Claire lets out a loud gasp, gaining the attention of anyone nearby.

'What are you saying, Magnus?'

'What I'm saying is you're not my mate. So our relationship needs to end. You're only going to get hurt if we stay together and I find my fated mate,'

'You're dumping me in front of everyone at school?'

'I suggested I talk to you privately,'

Claire bursts into tears.

'How dare you break up with me? No one breaks up with me!'

'Claire, I'm sorry, but it's over.' I take my textbook from my locker and head to English class.

She doesn't sit next to me in her usual spot but a few rows away, sobbing throughout the class.

'Claire, you have been crying throughout the class. It's rather distracting, you know. Do you need to see the school nurse?' A classmate asks.

'No, Magnus broke up with me.' Claire blurts out and cries louder.

All the girls in the class whisper amongst each other and smile at me. The bell rings, and I walk to my next class with a dozen girls following close behind. I completely ignore them and walk into science.

Nina sits at our wonky table in silence.

'Hey, Nina,'

'Hey,' she says quietly and focuses on the notes in her textbook.

'I thought maybe we could go to the library today and study up about curses. It might help us find out more about yours?'

'Shh, someone might hear you. I'll go to the library after school by myself. We need to avoid each other until you find your mate. I'm only sitting at this table with you because Mr Thomson made us lab partners, and we don't get a say in it.'

Knowing that Nina doesn't want to be around me after we already missed seven years of friendship is taking a toll on me. At lunch, I decide to spend it in the library and research curses to help Nina.

I've spent twenty minutes searching for a book about curses and cannot find one. I see Pipsqueak at her usual table.

'Psst, Pipsqueak,'

She looks around the library.

'Over here,' I whisper.

'Magnus?' She says, standing up from her chair as she approaches me. 'I-is everything alright?'

'I need your help,'

'W-what kind of help?'

'If I wanted to study curses, where would I find the right book?'

'Oh, curses or any type of magic isn't allowed, Magnus. Those books aren't out here with the other books. We would get in big trouble if we studied any kind of witchery, voodoo, or magic,'

'Where are they kept then?'

141

'In the t-town library, behind lock and key, in a r-room out of sight,'

'Do you know where?'

'Y-yes,'

'Great! Meet me at the town library after school,' I say, taking my leave.

'B-but...'

'4.pm sharp,' I yell out, 'And don't be late.'

The school bell rings. I run to my locker and take what I need. I shut my locker door to find Zak, May, and Josie standing there.

'Ready to go home, bro?' Flint says.

'Um, I have a school project I need to do. I'll be home late for dinner. Tell Mum and Dad not to worry about me.'

I run down the corridor, past Nina and Moss making out, and growl. They stop kissing and watch me continue running. My wolf wants to come out. Pain soars through my body. I stop running, lean on some lockers, and fight my wolf to contain itself. Once I'm in complete control, I race to the town library. Pipsqueak is waiting out the front.

'Are y-you okay, Magnus? Why are you drenched i-in sweat?'

'I'll be fine. I had to fight my wolf back,'

'Oh, so the r-rumours you have your wolf are t-true?'

'Yes,'

'Magnus, I know y-you want to see these books, but we will get into s-so much trouble. You should reconsider this,'

'No, I have to do this, Pipsqueak. I don't have any other choice,'

'Why? What has happened?'

'I can't tell you. Only the high-ranking wolves in the pack know, and I've been told not to tell anyone else,'

'Oh, Okay. I just m-might not be as much help if I don't know what it is you are trying to find the answer t-to,'

'For now, let's just get inside that room,'

Pipsqueak nods and gestures for me to follow her. We enter the library, and she leads me to the librarian's desk.

'See the office over there? Inside is another door at the back. It's locked, and that is where the forbidden books are,'

143

'Where is the key?'

Pipsqueak points at the librarian at her desk, scanning the box of returned books. I can see a ring of keys dangling by her side.

'How are we meant to get the keys when she is wearing them?'

'Y-you distract her. I'll sneak up behind her and take them,'

I nod my head and approach the librarian.

'Why hello, miss,' I say, gazing into the librarian's eyes.

'Yes, how can I help you?'

'I-I um was wondering if, ah, you fell from heaven?'

'Excuse me?'

'Well, heaven called and said they are missing an Angel, and I know a sweet angel when I see one,' I wink.

The librarian, twice my age, blushes while Pipsqueak facepalms herself.

'Oh, my,' she giggles.

I continue to flirt with her. Finally, pipsqueak successfully takes the keys and tiptoes into the back office.

'I'll see you around doll face.' I blow a kiss goodbye to the librarian. She sits down and fans her face as I walk away.

CHAPTER 18

Pipsqueak waves me over into the back of the office and unlocks the door. We step into the forbidden dark room together. It smells musty, and the many cobwebs show no one has been in here for years.

The structure differs from the rest of the library, which has plastered white walls, whereas this room has bluestone walls and old wooden beams across the ceiling. There are old rickety wooden bookshelves filled with old books. Some are leather-bound, and some have steel clasps and jewels on them. We approach the table carved from stone. There are a few small, half-melted candles, with some matches nearby. Pipsqueak lights the three candles. We stand side by side and take in the old medieval room.

'You start with those books, and I'll start with these,' I point.

'But I don't know what I'm looking for,'

'How to break a curse?'

'What are you getting m-me into?' she squeaks. I sigh and decide that I can trust her, and it's best to let her in on the secret.

'You can't tell anyone, okay?'

'O-okay,'

'It's Nina. Someone has cursed her, but we don't know what the curse is yet and how it affects her, and the curse is affecting me by making my shifts unbearably painful,'

'How do you know all this?'

'Because a witch came over and told us,'

'A witch? But they haven't existed in over a hundred years,'

'Sorry to break it to you, but they do. You can't tell anyone anything about any of this,'

'I won't tell, your secret is safe, but I have to ask if Nina is the one who has a curse, then how is it affecting you and not her?'

'That's just another reason we are here. We need to learn anything we can that will help,'

'Okay, well, we better get reading then.'

I take a book from one end of the bookshelf while Pipsqueak starts at the other end. I unlock the steel clasp and carefully flick through. Each page has a symbol and a description of what each represents and does.

Nothing helpful. I put it back and took the next book. I can't read it though it appears to be in Latin.

'Found anything yet?' I ask.

'No, this one seems to be about the history of witches from Salem. I'll keep looking.'

I glance at another book. The cover reads Spells and Hexes.

I run my fingers along with the words and read out loud.

'Casting spells or cursing ill-fortune on another comes with the cost of one's own curse. Only spells that mean well, will have no negative effect on the caster. Please proceed with caution,'

'What does that mean?' Pipsqueak asks. I shrug my shoulders and continue to read the book.

'Spells and hexes can be cast through many sources. Witches are the most popular known to cast spells and hexes. Spells cast in a group with their coven are longer lasting and harder to break. Arcane Mages work the same way as witches.

Anyone who knows how to use it can use relics. Items such as these can summon ghosts or even demons or may even curse someone. These could be items such as a voodoo doll, a small statue, or symbols made from twine or other materials. They usually place the item under the victim's pillow or bed if it's a curse.

Praying or wishing to one's God or Goddess may be granted if you are lucky. Anyone can also curse someone using their god's or goddess's name. A powerful sign will occur, such as an earthquake, lightning strike, or a loud rumble. If the god or goddess accepts your prayer, wish or curse,'

'Maybe you should check her bedroom for any relics when you return home?'

'That's a good idea,' I will try that.

I unzip my school bag and place the book inside.

'W-what are you doing, Magnus? You can't take the book. It would be -s-stealing,'

'I'm just borrowing it for now. I'll return it once we break the curse, okay?'

'I guess,'

'Time to get out of here.'

We blow the candles out and open the door ajar. Once the coast is clear, I walk out and distract the librarian again with more flirting while Pipsqueak locks up the room and returns the keys.

I give her a hi-five, and we part ways.

'See you at school tomorrow, Pipsqueak,'

'It's Pippa,' she yells behind me.

As soon as I return home, everyone is eating dinner.

'How did you go with your assignment?' Mum asks.

'I think I found some helpful information,' I say, walking up the stairs. I intend to go to Nina's room and search for any relics.

'Magnus, the rest of your assignment can wait. Join us for dinner. Your meal is already getting cold,'

'Okay, Mum,' I place my bag down. I'd prefer to search Nina's room first, but Zak, May, and Flint aren't aware of the curse, so I can't say why my meal can wait.

'What's the assignment for?' Dad asks.

'Um, it's for... science,'

'I didn't know we had an assignment,' Nina says.

I give her a "be quiet" look.

'Oh, you mean that assignment?' She says, catching on quickly.

I devour my meal so that they can excuse me from the table.

'What's the assignment about?' Her mother, Amelia, asks.

Nina looks at me for help.

'Weather, how different weathers form,' I say.

'Oh, fascinating,' she says.

'This dinner was delicious,' I say, walking around the table to Nina. I gently take her arm.

'Since I'm about to finish our assignment, you may as well come to help me,' I laugh nervously.

'Yes, our assignment,' she says, standing up and playing along. She knows I'm up to something. We reach the top of the stairs.

'What is going on with you, Magnus?'

'We have to search your room,'

'My room? What for?'

I look around to make sure no one is watching. I take Nina's hand, lead her into her room, and shut the door behind us. Unzipping my bag, I hand her the book of spells and hexes.

'Magnus, where did you get this? Do you know how much trouble we can get into for having this?'

'Yeah, I know. I'm just borrowing it for a while. I'll return it later,'

'You shouldn't have this,'

'Nina, I took it to help you,'

'How is this book going to help me?'

'Read this part here,' I tell her.

She gives me a confused look before reading.

'Relics. Items such as these can summon ghosts or even demons or may even curse someone. These could be items such as a voodoo doll, a small statue, or symbols made from twine or other materials. If it's a curse, they usually place the item under the victim's pillow or bed,'

Nina looks up from the book, 'Okay, and what's this got to do with anything?'

'We should search your room for any relics, just in case,' she smiles and nods, hopeful about my suggestion. Nina closes the book, places it in my bag and searches under her pillow and through her bedding.

'Nothing here,'

'Here, move aside. I'll lift your bed,' I walk over to Nina's big, bulky bed and lift it with ease. Nina moves the boxes of clothes aside that are underneath the bed.

'Nothing here,' she says.

'Check the boxes,' I say.

Nina tosses many items around. At the same time, I put the bed frame back down, lift the mattress, and check under it.

'Nothing,' I frown.

154

As she stands up, a loud knock at the door startles us. Nina slips, and I grab her with one hand and fall, holding the mattress with the other hand, and land huddled on the mattress together, our lips only an inch apart. The door opens. Zak, Flint, and May stand there with shocked, surprised looks while Nina and I yell out simultaneously.

'This is not what it looks like!'

CHAPTER 19

'So, it doesn't look like you two had a full-on make-out session that messed up Nina's bedroom. Even your mattress is on the floor,' Josie laughs.

I get myself off of Nina and help her up from the mattress on the floor.

'So, which one of you will explain this situation?' Flint asks.

Nina and I point at each other, and the others laugh.

'Well, we can't tell you,' I say.

'What do you mean you can't tell us?' Zak growls.

'Our Luna said we aren't to tell anyone else,' Nina explains.

'Who else knows about this secret thing you are keeping from us?' Zak asks.

'All our parents know, and then us two,' I say.

'So, our parents all know about whatever it is, but we aren't allowed to be let in on it?' Zak says.

'Correct,' I say, too guilty to look them in the eye.

'If you don't let us in on what is going on, I will tell everyone about you two making out,' Josie smirks.

Nina and I give each other a worried look.

'Fine, get in here and shut the door behind you,' I grumble.

Everyone finds a spot sitting on boxes. Nina and I sit on the mattress.

I lean over and grab the book and hand it to Zak first.

'We were searching Nina's room for any relics someone may have hidden here,'

'Relics? And why I am holding a book of Spells and Hexes!' Zak asks.

'I can't shift without it causing immense pain. So we had a witch named Yiselda come and see if she could figure it out,'

'A witch?' Josie says.

'Yes, there is a secret coven that still exists. Yiselda stated I can't shift without it causing immense pain because of a curse that Nina carries.'

'Nina's cursed?' Flint asks.

'Yes, we don't know what kind of curse or how it affects her, but it affects me. We can't break the curse without knowing who cursed her or what the curse is. So, Pipsqueak and I broke into the town's library secret, forbidden room to research curses. This book was the only one I had come across so far that may be helpful,'

'Wait, wait, wait, hold on a minute! There is a secret room in the library? And who is Pipsqueak?' Josie asks.

'Yes, the library keeps all the forbidden and banned books there. It was like a military operation to get in there without being caught. Pipsqueak is a friend from school. You all know her,'

Everyone gives each other a confused look. Zak passes the spellbook to Flint.

'I read in this book that curses can be made from relics and placed in bedrooms. So Nina and I searched her room when you guys knocked and startled us. Nina slipped, I caught her, and you all saw the rest,'

'Who would want to put a curse on Nina, though? It makes little sense,' Josie frowns.

'We don't know. We are trying to do what we can in the meantime to break it. No one else knows about this but our parents and Pipsqueak. Mother thinks Nina's life will be in danger if the pack finds out she is cursed, and it's affecting me, the future Alpha,'

Everyone gasps and stares at Nina with worry.

'I'll be fine as long as we keep this to ourselves, and besides, nothing has changed about me. It hasn't affected me yet, anyway,'

'If anyone notices anything that could be related to the curse, then let me know straight away.' I say.

Everyone nods, and we part ways and go to bed for the night.

I'm early for breakfast for the first time. Now pondering, I hadn't thought much about it until now. On your Eighteenth at midnight, we have our first shift and meet our wolves. The shift is involuntary, and the wolf takes over completely.

'Mum, Dad, if I already had my first shift, does that mean I won't shift at midnight tomorrow, or will I still involuntarily shift? I'm not supposed to shift. Remember to avoid the pain. Last time, I ended up with that terrible fever for days,'

Astrid and Ryker stare at each other and mind-link for a few minutes. Then, when they finish their private conversation, they look at me.

'We hadn't thought about the fact you might shift tomorrow night. Unfortunately, there isn't much we can do other than have the pack doctor nearby and wait,' Ryker says.

Flint and Josie enter the dining room. Astrid and Ryker change the subject, as they don't know Josie and Flint are aware of everything now.

'You might meet your mate as soon as today,' Astrid smiles.

'Yeah... Mum, maybe.' I say unenthused.

It should excite me that I can find my mate now, but I'm dreading it for some reason. I feel disappointed, and I don't understand why.

Nina enters the room and I can't help but smile when I see her. She gives me a small smile in return and sits down for breakfast.

My mother breaks my stare, addressing my attire.

'Surely, you're not wearing those clothes today when Alphas come to see you? They will bring their unmated daughters too, you know! So you must look your finest,' Astrid says.

Nina, May, Josie, and the boys try to contain their giggles.

'What's wrong with these jeans and this shirt?'

'Goodness Magnus, let's find something more presentable in your wardrobe.' Astrid stands and drags me up the stairs. Sometimes I wonder how she has so much strength in that tiny body. I assume being Luna strengthens her more than a regular she-wolf. Mum rummages through my wardrobe and hands me over suit pants with a white shirt and a maroon tie.

'Are you serious, Mum? It's not a ball,'

'No, it's not a ball. It's an even bigger event than that, my son. It's your eighteenth! Your wolf ceremony! Now get changed and get cracker-lacking this instance.' She orders and leaves my room.

I fall back onto my bed and lay there for ten minutes before getting dressed. I pull my black shoes out from under the bed and put them on. I come back down the stairs, and all eyes are on me.

'Now, that's more like it,' Astrid smiles.

I comb my hair back, using my fingers as Nina walks towards me. She smiles at me and steps that little bit closer. Our faces are near. She smiles, and I blush to wonder if she is about to kiss me in front of everyone. Instead, her hands reach up, adjusting my tie and placing a hand on my chest. 'There, that's better. Now you look perfect for your mate,' she says with a sad smile, 'I hope she is everything you dreamed of.' She says and walks away.

Staff bustle around the house, setting up decorations and a banquet for today's arrivals of guests. Alpha Mason arrives with his son, Hank, and two daughters, Bethany and Addison.

'Alpha Ryker, Luna Astrid, it's been far too long since we've seen each other,' he smiles.

'Alpha Mason, we are glad you could make it for our son's wolf ceremony,' Astrid says graciously.

'We wouldn't miss it, especially my two daughters. They have been dying to meet your son. Is he around perchance?'

I'm standing behind the statue of a giant knight behind the staircase, hoping no one sees me.

'Magnus, there you are,' Astrid smiles, finding me straight away as if she knows this is where I would be.

She leads me to our newly arrived guests. The daughters fan their faces and giggle.

'Oh, so handsome,' one says, and they both blush and giggle again.

'Magnus, these are my daughters, Bethany and Addison,'

I step forward and begrudgingly take Bethany's hand and place a kiss on the back of her hand and do the same with Addison. I know straight away neither of them is my fated mate.

'Pleasure to meet you both,' I say.

'And a pleasure to meet you too,' Bethany says with a curtesy.

'Yes, a pleasure,' Addison says, copying her sister's curtesy.

'And this is my son Hank, future Alpha of the Greystone pack,'

We make eye contact and shake hands as the front door opens; Nina enters.

'And who is that stunning, beautiful creatuuuure ough!' He yells, pulling his hand from my tight grip, 'You almost broke my hand?'

'Oh, did I? Oops, sometimes I forget my strength, forgive me.' I smirk.

CHAPTER 20

It's the night of my wolf ceremony. I spent the day with my parents, greeting all the Alphas who arrived and their families and pack members. It's been exhausting. I have met hundreds of unmated females who have swooned over me all day. Along with all that, I've been worried that I might shift against my will tonight. The pain I went through when I had shifted was unbearable, to the point I thought I would die. It's not an experience I want to repeat. I know the pack doctor is here just in case but is there anything he can do to help me?

More unmated she-wolves arrive and swoon around me. 'Is it true you shifted early? Is it true your wolf is white? Are your muscles real?' Another asks, feeling my biceps. I can't help but notice Nina glaring at me. She looks stunning in her red dress that flows at the bottom. It has a long slit on the right showing off her petite, beautiful legs. Her hair is up high, with a couple of strands dangling down her cheeks.

Great, what have I done to upset her now?

The Moon Hall has roughly a thousand people. I walk to take my seat. Moss arrives and takes Nina's hand, and sits beside her. Now I am the one glaring at her. Mum elbows me, gaining my attention.

'Not even one of these unmated she-wolves is your mate?' she asks with hope.

'No, Mother, I'm sorry,'

'It's okay. Perhaps your mate is not from any of these packs?'

'Patience, Mum, all in due time.'

She smiles, content with my answer. She nods.

My father stands up and thanks everyone for being here. Then, we enjoy the banquet over the next hour. Although I'm hungry, I don't feel like eating. So instead, I push my food around with my fork.

'It's time for the dance to begin.' My father announces. Mother elbows me to stand up. Because it's my wolf ceremony, I have to join the dance.

A dozen she-wolves try to outrun each other towards me, hoping for the first dance. I don't want to dance with them, but I have to oblige. Without looking, I take a hand and pull the she-wolf along to the dance floor. She giggles the whole time we dance. The song finishes, and I choose another random she-wolf and dance. She flutters her eyes the entire time, causing one of her fake eyebrows to fall off. She hasn't realised, and I say nothing. Moss and Nina approach the dance floor as I dance with the next girl.

I can't help but overhear everyone saying what a beautiful couple they make and that they hope they are fated mates. His hands seem to creep lower and lower every time I look, almost touching her ass. A growl erupts from within me. I can't control it. All eyes are on me. 'Sorry, everyone, my wolf wants to join the dance.' I joke, and everyone laughs and continues to dance. Moss holds Nina tightly against his body as they dance. I can't help but sense she is uncomfortable.

'Thank you for the dance,' I say politely to the girl and step away. I approach Moss and tap him on the shoulder, stopping their dance.

'As the future Alpha and being my wolf ceremony, it is only proper I get to dance with a girl of my choice,' I say, taking Nina's hand from his. He knows he can't decline as it will cause a scene and show disrespect to not only me but my father, the Alpha.

'Why certainly,' he snaps, clearly angry.

'Let me show you how it's done,' I smile at him.

Taking Nina's hand with my hand, I place the other gently on her waist and begin the waltz. I dance like a true gentleman, not allowing my hands to wonder.

'Are you okay?' I ask.

'Was it that obvious?'

'Yes, my wolf almost appeared when I saw where Moss's hands were going,'

'Well, that explains the growl that almost made the Moon Hall collapse,' she laughs, then has a serious expression, 'Are you nervous… that you might shift?'

'I won't lie, I'm nervous, but there is the chance I won't shift since I have had my first shift already,'

'That's true. I won't go anywhere, no matter what happens tonight, Magnus,'

'If I shift, will you… stay with me?'

'Of course, I will. I'll be right by your side.' She says, resting her head on my chest as we continue to slow dance. I want to stay like this forever, with my best friend in my arms where I can keep her safe and close to me forever.

Dad has the biggest grin, watching us as if he knows something I don't. I raise my eyebrow at him, and his smile only grows bigger.

'You were angry at me earlier. Did I do something wrong?' I ask.

'What do you mean?'

'Before the banquet when more she-wolves arrived, you glared at me?'

'Oh, I wasn't glaring at you. I was, never mind. It's not important. I was just being silly,' she says.

The dance ends. My hand drops from Nina's waist, and our hands slowly part even though they want to stay joined.

Moss approaches her quickly, takes her hand, and returns to their table. He looks over his shoulder and glares at me.

It's a quarter to midnight. My hands tremble, and I sweat as my wolf is trying to take over control. I'm trying with all my might to keep him at bay.

I am supposed to stand in the middle of the hall. There is a large round window on the ceiling for when the moon is in position to glow and shine over me.

'Magnus?' Astrid says, sensing something is wrong.

I look at her, and she gasps, startling dad and anyone nearby. My eyes are pure black, and sweat beads glide down my face.

'He is going to shift.' She says to Ryker with worry.

Dad and Leon place my arms over their shoulders and carry me to the moon's beam of light. I'm in a lot of pain.

I scream out as bones crack and break. My body flinches and flings around with each snap.

'Magnus!' I hear Nina yell. She runs towards me, but Moss grabs her arm and holds her back.

'No, you must stay here,' Moss tells her.

'No, I promised him I'll be by his side if he shifts,' she tells him.

'Nina, he is not your mate. It's not your business to intervene,' he growls.

'I don't care if he isn't my mate Moss, I-I-'

'You what?' He snaps.

'It doesn't matter. What matters is that I'm here, by Magnus's side,'

'You are to be by my side Nina, and you will stay by my side,' He grits through his teeth, taking her further back behind the crowd.

'Nin- argh!' My back snaps loudly right in the middle of my spine. The pack doctor kneels by my side.

Everyone whispers that the first shift is meant to be painful, but they have never seen a shift like this cause pain, almost to the point of death.

'Give him space, get back,' Astrid yells.

'Where is she?' I say.

'Where is who?' Astrid asks.

I can no longer speak. I can't reply as my arms and legs snap into place—white fur sprouts from my skin, and my face morphs. I howl so loud that it shakes the hall. I've shifted.

Everyone steps back and gasps or coos at my wolf's beauty and immense size.

My wolf only had one plan strictly on his mind: Moss.

My wolf growls ferociously, snarling as I leap over the frightened crowd.

Dad looks at my Mother.

'We need to shift now! His wolf has death on his mind, and we need to stop him.'

They shift quickly and race after me, leaving everyone confused.

My wolf is full of rage. How dare Moss take Nina away from me. I see nothing but red. I want to see nothing but blood, Moss's blood. I can sense wolves chasing after me, but their scent is familiar. I work out it's my parents following me.

My speed increases as I search for Nina and Moss. I sniff around and catch her scent of mint and lavender towards the parked cars. I howl, letting Moss know I'm after him. There is a car driving away. I know it's them. Before he gets too far, I leap onto the car's roof, causing Nina to scream and Moss to swerve.

'Let me out, let me go,' Nina screams at Moss.

'No, you are mine, Nina,'

'He will kill you, Moss!'

'Let him try.' He laughs.

Moss continues to drive, swerving, hoping I lose my grip and fall. Instead, I jump onto the car's bonnet and begin banging my head against the windshield. It cracks, then breaks, shattering into thousands of pieces.

Nina continues to scream and holds onto the car door. Moss speeds up even faster as I lunge forward into the car. I bite into his left arm, and Moss yells in pain. He swerves the car, and I slip, letting go of his arm. I jump back onto the car's roof as the car plummets full force into a tree. The impact tosses me a dozen metres away. Slowly standing on all fours, I gain my balance and look at the car smashed into the tree. Smoke rises from the bonnet.

Nina!

CHAPTER 21

I race towards the car. There is no sign of Moss. I can smell his scent in the woods. Nina is unconscious. Blood trickles down the left side of her head. There is glass everywhere.

I howl as loud as I can for help. Finally, Astrid and Ryker appear, shift into their human forms, and climb into the car.

'Where has Moss gone? You didn't kill him, did you?' Astrid asks worriedly. I shake my head and whimper as I step towards Dad carrying Nina.

'She needs to see the pack doctor right away. Otherwise, she might not make it.'

I lower myself down, knowing the quickest way to get her to the doctor is me taking her. Dad places her gently on my back and wraps her arms around my neck. I glide through the air like a bird with every leap, increasing my speed and making it a smoother run, so I don't drop her. My parents shift back into their wolves and can barely keep up with my pace. We arrive back at the ceremony. Everyone parted ways, screaming or startled at the sight of Nina.

'Nina!' Amelia screams.

Leon follows Amelia over to me. Nina's parents carefully lift Nina down, crying. The pack doctor assesses her.

'What happened to her?' Amelia asks me as my parents arrive and shift back.

'She was in a car accident. Moss was driving and fled the scene,' Astrid tells her.

'Let's get her into the packhouse where I can tend to her wounds.' The doctor says.

Leon carries Nina from the hall towards the packhouse.

'Thank you, everyone, for attending the ceremony, but it will have to end. So please enjoy the rest of your stay over the next few days.' Ryker says to all the guests.

They all leave and head to their cabins. Some of the she-wolves continue to try and get my attention. They want to touch me. I let out a slight snarl just for them to hear and watch as they cower back, changing their minds. I catch up with Leon and follow him up the stairs. He places her on her bed, and the doctor immediately attends to her wounds, cleans them, and bandages her. Nina lets out a whimper, even though she is still unconscious. I growl at the doctor, who quickly backs himself up to the wall.

'S-Sorry Magnus, I didn't mean to hurt her, but I must cleanse her wounds. She doesn't have her wolf yet, so she needs my help to heal properly,'

Amelia sits by Nina and holds her hand. Leon stands next to Amelia with a solemn look.

My parents enter the room.

'Magnus, aren't you going to shift back into human form?'

I shake my head and curl up by Nina's side. I'm going to stay here and protect her until she wakes. My head rests on her lap. Mum, Dad, and Nina's parents give each other a sad look, then look back at me and nod in understanding.

'You let us know when she wakes, ok, Magnus?' Leon says. I lift my head and nod, then resume my position on her lap.

I must have fallen asleep. The warmth from the sun beaming through the window warms my fur. Nina's hand is resting on my back. She hasn't woken but must have moved in her sleep. I move my position, rest my head on her pillow facing her, and fall asleep again. I wake up to a scream and sit up.

Nina and I are facing, sweat covers her forehead, and I watch as she realises it's just me.

'Magnus?'

I lick her face.

'Gross, Magnus!' She says. I whimper and lower my head and place my paws over my eyes. 'Sorry, Magnus, I didn't mean to growl. My head hurts,' she says, touching the patch on her left temple.

'Wait, last night. You were shifting. I tried to get to you, but Moss wouldn't let me. He dragged me into his car and sped off, then you jumped onto the roof, and that's all I remember. Did Moss crash the car?' She asks, observing the bandages down her arms and legs. I whimper again, but I sit up and rest my head on her lap this time.

She pats my head and glides her fingers through my fur. I'm in heaven.

'Thank you, Magnus, for rescuing me,'

Leon and Amelia barge into the room, panting.

'Nina, you're awake! We heard you scream,' Amelia says.

'Sorry, I didn't expect to wake up with an oversized wolf in my bed,' she laughs.

I whimper my apology, and she wraps her arms around my neck and pulls me in for a hug.

'It's okay, Magnus. I forgive you,'

'How are you feeling?' Leon asks her.

'I'm sore, but I think I'll be okay. Where is Moss?'

I growl at her question.

'We don't know. No one has seen Moss since he fled the car accident,' Leon says.

'What if he's hurt?'

I growl again. Why should Nina care if Moss is hurt?

'I know you're not fond of him, Magnus. I know he should not have taken me away like that, but I think he was worried about me,'

Not wanting to hear anymore, I step off the bed and go to my room. After ten minutes of excruciating pain, I shift back and pass out from the exhaustion and pain.

I'm woken by Zak and Flint shaking my shoulders and tapping my face.

'I'm okay now,' I say, sitting up.

'Is it going to be this bad every time you shift?' Zak asks.

'Yup, at least until Nina's curse has been broken,'

I make myself presentable and walk downstairs with Flint and Zak. We find Hank the Greystone packs future Alpha looking around.

'Hank, can I help you?' I ask.

'Actually, you can. I have a proposition to offer,' Hank smirks.

'What kind of proposition?'

'One, you would prefer we speak about privately,'

'Whatever you need to say to our future Alpha, you can say to us,' Flint says.

'Well, if you don't mind everyone finding out about Nina's curse? I'd hate to know what would happen to her if anyone found out,'

I grab him by the scruff of the neck and growl in his face. My eyes have turned black. I quickly let him go as people enter the room.

'Flint, Zak, gather Josie, May, and Nina. We are to meet by the lake immediately.'

We all leave and promptly arrive by the lake.

'What's going on?' Josie asks.

'Hank knows about Nina's curse. He has some proposition to make. I assume in return for him to keep his mouth shut?' I say, glaring at Hank.

'How did he even find out?' May asks.

'None of us have told anyone, though?' Flint says and looks at us all. Nina hugs herself and looks down.

'Nina, what is it?' I ask.

'I-I thought I could trust him. I thought he could help me find out how to break this stupid curse,' she cries.

183

I pull her into my chest and let her cry.

'Who is him?' Josie asks.

'Moss,' Hank and I say at the same time.

'Shit,' Zak says.

'Why did he tell you?' I ask Hank.

'Moss and I go way back. We went to Pup school together far South from here. So, you could say we are very close friends. In case anything happened to him, he told me to tell his mother about the curse,'

'What good would telling his mother about the curse do?' I ask.

'I don't know, but I know my sisters are inconsolable now that neither of them isn't your mate. My father expected one of them to at least be your mate and was quite frustrated himself when he realised they weren't,'

'Yes, I get it. I broke the hearts of hundreds of other she-wolves last night. So what's your point?'

'My point or proposal, I shall say, is that my father still wants to find a way for you to be mated with one of his daughters, and now I have leverage over you. I have a way for it to happen,' he smirks.

184

'Excuse me?' I growl.

'I won't tell anyone about Nina's curse, and in return, you choose one of my sisters to be your mate,'

'What!? Are you crazy? I can't just choose a mate. I need to find my fated mate!'

'Nonsense. It may be unusual to choose a mate rather than wait for your destined mate, but I've known plenty of wolves who have had chosen mates, and most have had a reasonably happy life,'

'My parents would never allow me to have a chosen mate,'

'Well then, you better not let them know and pretend one is your fated mate,'

I grind my teeth and fall to my knees in pain. My wolf is trying to take over and shift so he can kill Hank.

'Magnus!' Nina yells and kneels beside me.

Her touch helps calm my wolf.

'You can't do this, Hank. You can't force me into mating one of your sisters,'

'I won't force you, Magnus. You will choose to do it to save your friend. If I let it slip, she has a curse. We all know they will hunt her down and kill her even by members of your pack,'

My wolf growls, and I yell in pain again. Zak and Flint help me stand. Nina gives me a worried look.

'You can't do this, Magnus. You can't choose one of them and pretend she is your fated mate! I can pack my stuff and leave Shadow Crest right now. I could never live with myself if you had to live with and mate with someone you didn't want to be with,'

'No, I could never live with myself if you ever left Shadow Crest… left… me. No matter where you go, someone would also be after you until they found and killed you,'

'Then what do we do?' She cries.

Flint, Zak, Josie, and May all have worried looks on their faces.

'I will do anything it takes to protect you, Nina.'

CHAPTER 22

'Which sister is the oldest?' I ask.

'That would be Addison,' he smiles.

'You can't be seriously thinking about doing this, Magnus?' Josie says.

'What other choice do we have?'

Josie glares at Hank, 'We could kill him?'

'Josie, that would only worsen the situation, especially if the evidence is led back to us as the killers,'

Hank is looking at us, mortified that murdering him could be an option.

'If you ever tried to kill me, Moss would know you were all behind it,'

He is right, but I already knew killing him wouldn't help the situation.

'What if your sisters want to find their fated mates?' I ask.

'Please, Magnus, we all know you're a catch and going to be one of the best, and strongest Alpha's in the land, and with a pure white wolf, any she-wolf would give their fated mate up in a heartbeat,'

'I need time to consider this. At least give me that?'

'Fine, I will inform my father and Addison of the proposal in the meantime and that you will consider it, but I won't mention Nina's little curse to them... for now, anyway,' he smirks.

'Let's go home.' I say to everyone.

We return home and meet in Nina's bedroom.

'We need to all brainstorm a way out of this. Otherwise, I will have no choice but to have a mateship with Addison,'

Everyone nods as my mother knocks on the door.

'Time for dinner, everyone,' she yells.

'Okay,' we shout back.

We all walk downstairs and join our parents for dinner.

'I hope you have been taking it easy today, sweety?' Amelia asks Nina.

'Of course, Mother,' she forces a smile.

'You lot are extra quiet tonight,' Ryker says.

'It's just been a long weekend, Dad. After all, it was my wolf ceremony, and Nina was in a car accident,'

'That's true. Seth was able to speak with Moss today,' he says. We all give each other a surprised look and stare back at my dad to speak, 'He had some cuts and bruises, but otherwise, he is fine. Moss said Nina and him left the ceremony of their own will as it was too much for Nina to watch Magnus shift. When he saw he was being chased and attacked by your Magnus, he freaked out, causing the car to crash. Moss knew you were only there to bring harm to him and not Nina, hence why he left Nina, knowing she would receive immediate care. He thought it best to flee for his safety and to not take the need for medical attention off Nina by him being there,'

'Well, that explains that,' Astrid says.

'Are you saying that Magnus is the one that put my daughter in danger and not Moss?' Leon growls and glares up at me.

The room goes silent. Nina tries to speak, but the words don't come out.

'I would never intentionally put Nina in danger. She was supposed to be there while I shifted, and Moss wouldn't allow her to stay,'

'Even so, Magnus, that's no reason to hunt someone down! The car accident would never have happened if you never went after Moss in the first place,' Leon growls.

'If Moss hadn't taken her away from me, it would not have happened,' I growl.

'Magnus, you will soon be the Alpha once you find your mate. Your selfishness and recklessness have me worried that you might jeopardise this pack,'

'How dare you speak that way to me, your future alpha,'

'How dare you endanger my daughter's life!'

My dad slams his fist on the table, silencing us both.

'Leon! Magnus! You both need to stop this. This was an accident, and thankfully Nina will be alright,'

'Please, Dad, Ryker is right. It was an accident. Magnus would never do anything to hurt me,' Nina says.

Leon and I look down in guilt for upsetting her.

'I'm sorry, Magnus, I couldn't imagine my life without Nina,'

'I'm sorry too. I also could never imagine my life without Nina,' I reply.

We both give each other a slight nod to accept each other's apology.

Nina smiles at us both.

'Thank you, Daddy,' I hear her whisper.

We eat in silence and welcome the change of topic.

'Zak, you will have your wolf in a few weeks, then Nina will get hers a few weeks after that. Are you both excited?' my mother Astrid asks.

'You bet. I can't wait to meet my wolf and start my search for my lifelong mate,' Zak smiles.

'Yeah, I'm excited to meet my wolf and be able to join in on hunts and border patrol duties. I feel nervous and on edge about meeting my mate, though,' Nina says.

'Why so nervous about it, sweety?' Amelia asks.

'I don't know why mum,' she whispers and momentarily glances my way.

'Not to worry, sweety. I'm sure whoever your mate is will treat you like a Queen,'

'Thanks, Mum.' Nina smiles.

The following day, I get ready for school as I step outside the front. I'm face to face with Alpha Mason, who seems rather happy.

'Good morning, Alpha Mason,'

'Magnus, I was hoping to have a quick private chat with you?'

'Um, sure,' I say. We walk towards the trees, away from the packhouse.

'My son Hank came to me with wonderful news last night that you would highly consider choosing Addison as your future mate and Luna? I had to ask you if you were serious about this?'

I do not want to be with Addison at all. I want to be with my fated mate and keep Nina safe from harm's way, but I can't tell him that. But I think I know how to give myself more time to meet my fated mate.

'Yes, Hank came to me with the idea that since I'm to take over as Alpha, I won't have the luxury of waiting years to find my fated mate. If I were not to find my mate by my nineteenth, my pack would become unsettled, and I would have to consider a chosen mate. Although my parents would disapprove of it, I would have to pretend Addison is my fated mate,'

'So, what you are saying if you haven't found your mate within a year, you will choose Addison as your mate?'

I want to say no. I want to scream no from the rooftops, heck, from the top of the mountains!

'Yes,' I say casually.

'Very well, Magnus, it is agreed then. One year to find your fated mate. If your mate isn't found by then, you will take Addison as your mate?'

With great hesitation, I nod.

Nina, Josie, Zak, and Flint exit the house together. Their faces go from smiles to frowns when they see me conversing with Alpha Mason.

'I need to go. My friends are waiting for me,' I say.

'I'll see you around... future son-in-law.' He chuckles.

An eerie shiver trickles down my spine at his words.

'Let's go,' I say to the others.

'What was that about?' Flint asks.

'I made a deal with Alpha Mason. It's not ideal or what I want, but it's a better deal than Hank's and gives us more time to get out of it,'

'What deal? Magnus, please don't tell me you agreed to anything you will regret?' Nina says with sorrowful eyes.

'I have one year to find my fated mate. If I don't, I'm to take Addison as my mate. Which also gives us a year to break Nina's curse. If we ever figure out what it is,' I retort, kicking a rock into the distance.

'What will Hank say when he finds out you've extended the deal?' Josie asks.

'Well, the deal is still on. I've just gotten more time out of it. Hank probably expected me to take Addison as my mate within a few days. Of course, he will be annoyed, but he will get over it,'

'I hope so,' Josie frowns.

CHAPTER 23

Claire spends the day following me around at school.

'Boo-boo, I was hoping we could talk?'

'Stop calling me Boo-boo, and I'll give you five minutes to talk to me,'

'Oh, okay then, B-Magnus...' she trails off.

I lean against my locker with my arms crossed.

'What is it?'

'I was hoping you would reconsider... us? I want us to be together again. Magnus, I miss you,' she says, trying to caress my bicep.

'I'm not interested, Claire,'

'But I don't want to be with anyone else,'

'Claire, you say that now, but you will eventually meet your mate and want to be with him. I'm going to be late for class. I'll see you around.'

Claire's eyes well up, and she storms off to her class.

At lunchtime, I head to the library and pull Pipsqueak aside.

'I heard about what happened at your wolf ceremony. Are you alright?'

Of course, the entire school would know about it.

'Yeah, I'm fine, but I need to update you on everything else. Nina told her boyfriend, Moss, about the curse. He has told his friend Hank, and now Hank is using it against me to choose his sister as my mate. I spoke with his father, Alpha Mason. I stretched the agreement to a year until I have no choice but to choose Addison as my mate. Otherwise, Hank will tell everyone about Nina's curse, which puts her in danger of being hunted down and killed. So, I have one year to break the curse, which will also get me out of the mateship agreement,'

'I see,' she says, pushing her thick glasses closer to her eyes. 'And we still have no clue what the curse is? Did you find any relics or symbols in her bedroom?'

'No, we tore the room apart and found nothing,'

'So, we can rule out that type of curse, then? What was another way to curse someone? Didn't it mention by a witch or a Mage?'

'Yes, but I don't think mages exist anymore, and there is only one witch I know of, and she had never met Nina before the day she came to see me,'

'I guess the only thing we can do is wait for the curse to affect her to give us any clue or lead to work on,'

'What if that doesn't happen for years to come?'

'Then you will have no choice but to accept Addison as your mate,' she says.

I look away and drop to the floor with my back against the wall. My hands cover my face as I panic—pain sears through my body. My wolf is fuming at the thought of having a chosen mate. He tries to take over and shift.

'Magnus!' Pipsqueak yells. She tries to calm me down, but I only growl at her touch. She trembles and takes a few steps back.

'I'm going to find someone to help. I'll be right back, Magnus. Whatever you do, don't shift.'

Everyone is panicking and fleeing the library. Pipsqueak disappears into the crowd. The entire school can probably hear my screams of pain. There is no use fighting my wolf anymore. I'm exhausted and barely conscious.

I stand on all fours and sway for a moment from exhaustion. My wolf exits the library and enters the school corridor. Anyone in the corridor quickly runs into the nearest classroom and locks the door.

Dozens of students stare out the windows. They tremble at the fierce size of my wolf with my large snarling teeth on show. I have no control over my wolf. He won't listen to me.

'I know you want your mate, and we will find her one day, but we need to keep Nina safe,'

He lets out a ferocious growl. He has picked up a scent. I realise it's Moss's scent.

'We can't harm Moss, and I know you hate him. I hate him too, but we are the future Alpha of this pack. We can't go around killing someone just because we don't like them,'

My wolf ignores me and is now in pursuit, following the scent up the corridor. He stops at a locked door and howls. Moss is in the room.

My wolf repeatedly rams into the door.

'Magnus?' Nina says behind me. Pipsqueak is next to her.

My wolf nods his head, letting her know he is in control.

'I know Magnus can hear me. You need to give him back control,' Nina says.

My wolf growls low.

Nina steps closer and kneels in front of my wolf, something no one else would dare do, not even Pipsqueak. She is so courageous, facing my fierce, unpredictable wolf like this. Her fingers caress the fur on my face and glide down my back. My wolf whimpers and lowers himself down, and rolls onto his back.

Nina giggles as she scratches my belly.

No one can believe their eyes. We aren't mates, yet she can control my wolf. It is unheard of and nothing anyone has seen before. I sit up, and she wraps her arms around my neck. My wolf has completely calmed and completely forgotten Moss is only meters away.

My wolf is giving me some control back. I lower myself and whip my head around, gesturing for Nina to hop on my back. I want to take her somewhere, do something special for her.

With no hesitation, she smiles and climbs onto my back. I'm so large it's like she is on horseback. I run back down the corridor and out of the school grounds with great speed, even faster than Nina could ever run. She screams with excitement as she holds onto the thrilling ride. We glide through the woods to the mountaintop. I let out a vast, dominant howl. Anyone that can shift does so and howls in return as a sign of respect. Nina spends an hour on my back. I don't stop, and I don't slow down. My wolf is so happy to be running free with Nina. He hasn't even thought about our fated mate and is content. We finish our run by the lake. I run and thrash through the water. My fur is soaking wet. Nina swims around and laughs when I shake my body, causing droplets to splash onto her.

'Magnus,' she laughs.

My wolf collapses with happiness on the grass. The sun shines over me and dries my fur. Nina wrings the water from her shirt and sits with her back against my belly.

'I have never had so much fun, Magnus. You ran faster than I could even run. Wasn't it the best feeling? It was so thrilling and so much fun?' She turns her head to see my response but sees a giant sleeping wolf passed out from exhaustion. She snuggles up to me and falls asleep.

Hours go by, and I wake up dry to find Nina asleep against me. I spend the next half an hour silently watching her sleep until she wakes up.

Her eyes open, and her lips grow wide with a smile. She sits up and pats me gently.

'You're going to have to shift back, you know. Did you want to do it now while I'm here or privately back home?'

Even though it will be excruciating either way, it's easier when Nina is with me. I focus my mind and whimper. She knows I'm going to shift now. The pain is horrendous, but her touch helps soothe me through the process. I sit up in my human form, thoroughly drenched and weak.

Nina throws her arms around my neck and hugs me. I place my hands on her back and make the most of the moment, knowing I will never get to hold her like this again once I'm mated.

'Let's go home.' She smiles.

She helps me stand, and we trudge home. She has my arm over one shoulder, so I don't fall. As soon as we arrive home, Leon and Seth quickly take me from Nina and help me to my room, where I pass out for the rest of the day and night.

CHAPTER 24

'He needs to stop shifting. What if one of these shifts kills him?' Astrid cries as I come down the stairs.

'Mum, please, I had no control over the shift. My wolf wouldn't listen to me, even after we shifted,'

'You realise if you have no control over your wolf and you are shifting against your own will and your wolf's only plan is to kill people, the council will demand you be locked up in the dungeon. Not only that, you may lose your rank as Alpha, and they would then give it to Flint,' My father says in a severe tone. 'They have already summoned me to see them today, probably because you almost attacked school students yesterday,' Ryker says, slamming his fist on the table. He falls back into his chair and rests his forehead in his hand in frustration.

'But I didn't attack anyone. No one got hurt,'

'You were going to attack someone, though. Students stated you were trying to break down a door to get into a classroom. You terrified everyone at the school. If it weren't for Nina, you would have hurt or, even worse, killed someone. And how Nina could calm your wolf without being your fated mate is an absolute mystery. People are spreading rumours that she must be delving into witchery or magic to tame and ride your wolf. I told them Nina is into no such thing and to not spread misinformation about her, but I fear the rumours will spread, anyway,'

'What do we do?' I ask.

'I think you and Nina can stay home and school here for the next couple of weeks until the rumours stop spreading,'

I nod in agreement.

Seth had set up two desks for Nina and me in the packhouse. Dad thought Seth would be best at being our teacher. But unfortunately, he was the most boring teacher and would drag on for hours, talking about the same topics. I scrunched up a piece of paper and threw it at the back of his head. Nina and I laugh but stop when he turns around, unimpressed.

'Which one of you threw that?' Nina and I both shrug and try to hold in our laughs.

Later on, we made paper airplanes and threw them in the air. They flew and crashed into the whiteboard.

'Are you two going to listen to the lesson and learn something or not? This is the last semester of the year until you both graduate.' He huffs.

Almost two weeks after Seth's gruelling home-schooling goes by. It's now the weekend of Zak's wolf ceremony.

'I think it will be okay for you to return to school on Monday,' Ryker says.

'Thank goodness, Dad. I don't think I could handle any more lessons from Seth,' I laugh.

'Me either,' Nina says. 'I'll see you at the ceremony tonight,' she waves.

'Wait, where are you going?' I ask.

'I um… I'm going to see Moss,'

'What! But why?'

'We haven't spoken to each other ever since your ceremony. I was going to talk to Moss at school that day about some things, but you shifted, and we haven't been back at school since. Moss wants to speak to me, and I want to talk to him before seeing him at the ceremony tonight,'

'Do you want me to come with you?'

Nina bursts into laughter.

'Because that would go down so well, wouldn't it?'

'Fine, I'll see you at the ceremony tonight,'

She hugs me goodbye. I decide to hang out with Josie, Flint, and Zak.

'I can't believe it's my first shift tonight!'

'You must be thrilled. I still have to wait another year,' Flint mumbles.

'At least you don't have to wait two years like me,' Josie pouts.

'That's true,' Flint replies.

'Zak, are you okay if I invite my friend Pipsqueak to attend the ceremony?'

'Sure, although I don't know who that is,'

'Cool, thanks,' I say.

It's time for the ceremony. Pipsqueak is running late, and I haven't seen Nina yet.

The banquet is ready, and we all take our seats.

'Mum, Dad, have you seen Nina?'

'Not since around lunchtime,' Ryker says.

'No, I've been busy helping prepare the ceremony all day,' Astrid says.

Leon and Amelia join us at the table.

'Is Nina on her way?' I ask them.

They give each other a morbid look.

'No, we thought she was here with you already?' Amelia says.

'She was with me at lunch and said she was going to meet up with Moss to talk things out, and then she would be here for the ceremony,'

'Maybe they are busy making out?' May jokes as she sits next to Amelia. Everyone gives her the 'really?' look.

'What, I'm serious. They were pretty friendly when I saw them at the park earlier today?'

'What do you mean?' I ask.

207

'They were sitting at the park bench talking, and Moss had his arm over the back of the seat where Nina sat. I didn't stop to chat, though. I figured Nina would accuse me of spying on her, and she still hasn't been talking to me,' May frowns.

'We will give her a little more time until we send out warriors to search for her then.' Leon says.

We have finished eating and are becoming worried. Zak takes his spot under the moon's light and begins his shift.

His shift is much quicker and smoother than mine was. He is in wolf form within a few minutes and lets out a howl. Seth and Mia shift and race through the woods. Pippa finally arrives, panting and struggling for breath. I quickly catch her before she falls.

'Nina, gone, taken, tried to help her, got here soon as could,'

'What?' Leon and I say in unison.

'Did you say Nina's been kidnapped?' Leon asks.

She pushes her glasses up towards her eyes, nodding.

'Yes, Moss took her,'

The colour from Leon's face drains.

Zak returns from the run, sniffing the air and wagging his tail. He shifts instantly into human form and runs up to Pipsqueak, panting for air, lifting her, and holding her tight against his chest.

'Mate!' He says, squeezing her so tight she whimpers, and her glasses fall.

'Zak, I need to speak with Pipsqueak urgently,' I tell him.

'Mine!' He snarls, holding her tight.

'Pipsqueak?' Josie says, 'That's Pippa, you idiot,'

'Whatever, we don't have time for name games. Moss kidnapped Nina, and we need to know which way they have gone,'

'S-south,' Pipsqueak manages to say.

Zak kisses her face and neck a hundred times, causing her to blush as red as a beetroot.

'T-that T-tickles.' She laughs at him.

Leon and I run from the ceremony hall and then stop to brief each other.

'You can't shift into your wolf, Magnus. I suggest we go south by car. Otherwise, you won't be able to keep up.'

He is right. I nod, and we run towards the packhouse.

Seth, mind links the pack warriors to head south and begin tracking Nina.

While I jump into the passenger seat of his car, he speeds off into the distance. In the distance, we can see the warriors in their wolf forms spread out searching.

'If he lays one finger on my sister, I'll kill him,' May growls in the back seat.

Leon slams on the brakes.

'May, what are you doing here? Go back to the packhouse,'

'No, I've never been there for Nina when she has needed me. I've been a terrible sister to her, to the point she doesn't even talk to me anymore. But she needs me now more than ever, and I'm going to help save her whether I come with you or go on my own.' She growls at her Dad.

'You better buckle up then.' Leon says and speeds ahead.

CHAPTER 25

It's 3 am. We have driven through the major city. We have been driving with the windows down to keep track of Nina's scent. Leon is growing weary and tired.

'Leon, maybe I should drive for a while?'

'No, Nina's scent is becoming fainter. We don't have time to pull over, not even for a moment. The last time I came through this city to track down a scent was to find your mother after Alice, our old cook, threatened to kill her,'

'Why would the cook threaten to kill my mother?'

'Her daughter Vanessa was in love with your father and was to become his chosen mate and Luna. He didn't love Vanessa, though. The council forced the arrangement onto him, and everything changed when he met your mother. He was so happy to have found your mother, Astrid. I remember when she wouldn't believe we were werewolves or that they existed. Jim from the diner shifted in front of her, and boy, did she cry wolf! The Diner was a mess after that. We found your mother in Shady Crest. Alpha Zenith had been keeping her prisoner in his dungeon and was going to make his son mark her. He had also captured Seth when he was looking for your mother in the city and placed him in the cells with her. That's where I met Amelia, my mate. She was down there as well,'

'Mum was a prisoner at Shady Crest?' May says, bewildered.

'Yes, she was. We were able to free them all just in time, as Astrid had her first shift. Any longer, and it would have been too late, as Alpha Zenith's son would have marked and mated her.'

Dad had an arranged mateship against his will, just as I currently have, but then he met Mum just in time to break the arrangement. Now, ironically, I'm in the same boat. I just have to break Nina's curse.

'Damn, I can't smell her scent anymore,' Leon says.

He pulls over and shifts into his wolf, and sniffs around. May and I step out of the car. Although we can pick up scents, it is much easier in wolf form. He mind-links the warriors.

'They have also lost her scent and have spread out further to cover all tracks,' Leon tells us.

'Should we spread out too?' May asks.

'No, if we continue south, we will eventually hit snowy weather, and we won't be able to pick up anyone's scent and may become lost. Let's follow this road South for now, and hopefully, we will pick her scent up again along the way.'

By 8 am, we are half asleep. Leon swerves the car as he falls asleep.

'Leon!' I yell, grabbing the steering wheel. He wakes up and quickly puts his foot on the brake.

'We are no good, dead to Nina. We have no choice but to sleep, then continue searching for her.' May yells.

213

Neither of us argues with her. May is right.

Leon pulls over, and we sleep in the car and wake in the afternoon.

'We should eat,' May says.

'No, we should get driving and find Nina,'

'Dad! You need to eat. We all do. What good are we if we are weak when we find her and need to fight?'

Leon stays silent as he drives to a diner.

'Eat quickly.' He says.

We nod, walk in, and place our order.

I inhale my massive pile of eggs and bacon down. At the same time, May inhales a stack of fifteen pancakes swimming in golden syrup.

Leon eats the breakfast platter with baked beans, bacon, toast, and mushrooms.

As soon as we finish eating, we head to the car. I take over driving while Leon sticks his head out the window and tries to pick up Nina's scent. We spend all afternoon and half the night driving. Panic is building up inside me as I fear for Nina's safety.

I pull over just in time as my eyes turn black, and I yell in pain.

'His wolf Dad! We have to stop him from shifting,' May says as she jumps out of the back seat and opens up the driver's side. It's dark, but being werewolves, we can see well. May holds my hand.

'Think of Nina, think of all the fun times you had. The swims in the lake, the trees you climbed, the time she filled the washing machine with bubble bath,'

My wolf calms, and I burst into laughter at the memory.

'It wasn't Nina who filled it with bubbles. It was me. It was always me doing the wrong thing. Yet she always took the blame. She was always protecting me,' I confess.

'Nina got into so much trouble because of that,' Leon growls.

'I suppose now is the time to confess. I also broke May's window and hid in her closet. Nina was with me, but she didn't hide. Instead, she again took the blame,' A terrible feeling washes over me.

'Nina, please be okay,' I say, staring at the moon.

Something whacks my head.

'Ow!' I look up at May.

'That's for breaking my window,' she whacks me again.

'Ow!'

'That's for letting Nina take the blame,'

She goes to whack me across the head again.

'And this one is for you to snap out of it and pull yourself together,'

Leon grabs her wrist in time.

'That's enough, May. He has learned his lesson and feels guilty for it,'

May sighs, 'You're right. Let's get some sleep and continue our search when we wake.'

We fall asleep and wake up mid-morning.

Leon Mind-Links the warriors and my Dad. There has been no sighting of Nina or Moss.

Dad mind-links me. He wants me to return home.

'No, I'm not returning home until Nina is safe.' I block the mind link before my Dad can argue with me.

We stop at a petrol station and fill up the tank. May and I grab as many packets of chips, snack bars, and water as we can carry and pay for it with the fuel.

As we approach the next town, snow covers the fields.

'We might have to stay in this town until we have a lead to follow,' Leon says.

'We can't stop looking for Nina,' I say.

'We won't stop looking for her, but we have no leads and no idea where we are going but South. They could have changed directions at some point and gone East or West, leading us further away from her.'

He has a point. We find a motel and go to the nearest clothes store to buy a snow jacket, socks, boots, and anything else to keep us warm in the snow. We spend four days entering every store and asking every person if they have seen Nina. Leon shows them a photo of her. Everyone apologises and says they haven't seen her.

Dad tells Leon it's been over a week, and we should return home. He has let all the Alphas of all the other packs know Moss has kidnapped Nina. They will let him know if there are any sightings of Nina or Moss.

'Your father is ordering us to return home. However, I won't be returning until I find Nina. So perhaps you two should consider going home?'

'No!' May and I shout.

'We are staying. We won't return either until we find Nina,' I growl.

'Let's drive to the next town and ask locals if they have seen Nina.' May says.

We spend four hours driving to the next town. It's just as cold as the previous town.

May and I are in the back seat, hovering our hands over the car heater. Our breath is foggy from the cold air.

'Do you think Moss is looking after her?' May sobs.

'If he truly cares for Nina, he would not have kidnapped her. I hope she is okay and that she knows we won't give up on her,'

'It's her eighteenth next week. If we haven't found her by then, maybe she will shift and be able to fight Moss and free herself?'

'May, I don't think I could go another day without her.'

CHAPTER 26

As soon as daylight arrives, we hit the streets and show a photo with Nina in it.

'Excuse me, sir, have you seen this girl?'

'No, sorry,'

'Excuse me, miss, have you seen this girl?'

'No, I haven't,'

We are just about to call it a day when an older lady looks harder at the photo.

'I haven't seen the girl you are looking for, but I have seen him,' she says, pointing to Moss standing behind Nina in the photo.

'Are you sure? When and where did you see him?' I ask.

'Moss, I think his name is. He is the future Alpha of a pack of ruthless, mongrel rogues,'

'He's a future Alpha?' I say, in complete shock.

'Yes, his mother is well known around here too, and not for good reasons. Their pack members are always stealing from all the surrounding towns and villages. They also kidnap she-wolves and force mateships between those she-wolves and their rogues,'

May, Leon, and I look at each other in shock at what we are being told.

'We have to tell Alpha Ryker,' Leon says and mind-links him immediately.

'Where does the pack live?' I ask.

'They live in the woods amongst caves that link together. It's about a one-hour drive south from here,'

A few she-wolves walk past us, giggling, and one winks at me.

'Shoo, shoo!' May yells and chases after them.

I try not to laugh, but I appreciate her scaring them away. Finding my mate is the last thing on my mind. The only thing that could make me truly happy is finding Nina and bringing her back home.

'Ryker said he will organise warriors from packs near our location to help us free Nina and any other she-wolves he has,'

'That could take hours, days even!' I growl, 'We need to go now,'

The woman laughs.

'Finding her isn't as simple as it sounds. First, you will need to bring someone with you that knows where their hidden traps are and which caves are the right ones to go through. You will be lost forever if you go down the wrong cave,' she cackles.

'Couldn't you show us?' May asks.

'I could, but I might be growing too old for these adventures,'

May looks her up and down and takes her arm.

'You don't look a day over fifty-nine,' she smiles, 'Now hop in. You're coming with us,' May says, holding the car door open.

'What's your name?' I ask the woman.

'Mabel,' she smiles.

'I'm...'

'Magnus, May, and Leon. Am I right?'

'How do you know that?'

Mabel ignores my question and points up ahead.

'Take the second left from there,' she says.

Leon takes the left turn and drives for roughly twenty more minutes.

'The rest of the way will have to be on foot. No car gets through those trees,' Mabel says, pointing towards the woods.

May grabs a backpack from the car and puts a few snack bars and bottles of water inside.

'Ryker wants us to wait for backup,' Leon says.

'We need to find Nina and assess the situation. If it's not safe, we will wait for backup,' I say.

Everyone nods.

Once we enter the woods, Mabel picks up a thick, long branch.

'You will all need one of these,' she says.

'What for?' Leon asks as she uses it in front of her as if she were blind. We hear a snap sound. Mabel pauses.

'This is why,' she smiles.

A log tied to rope comes swinging down, missing Mabel by inches.

'Woah!' May says.

'Use the branches to activate any traps. Stop as soon as you hear any sound, and step back until the trap is active. Then you can continue around it,'

'Clever,' Leon says, finding himself and May a branch.

I look around and take a perfectly placed branch off the ground. As I pick it up, I'm yanked back by the old lady just as wooden spikes pop up from the ground in front of me.

'Not that branch,' she smirks.

I stare back at the branch that has a rope tied around it. As I picked it up, it pulled the rope, activating the spikes that were supposed to penetrate my chest. I take a less obvious branch and begin gliding it across the ground in front of me. We follow Mabel's lead. She has been here before.

'This way,' she says for the fiftieth time.

At this rate, the warriors will be there before us.

Mabel laughs.

'What's so funny?' I ask.

'Nothing, nothing at all,' she says with a bemused look.

'There's a cave over here,' May says.

'Not that one, dear,' Mabel says.

'But it looks safe, and there's plenty of light there,'

'Ah, to be young and naïve,' Mabel says.

'And what is that supposed to mean, lady?' May huffs.

'It means you're young and dumb, my dear,'

I cover my mouth and cannot contain my laugh for my life. The look on May's face is priceless.

'Why, you old crone!' May says, about to throw a stone at her.

Her dad grabs her wrist just in time.

'May, she's old. You know to respect your elders,' Leon growls at her.

'But... she started it!'

'May, I don't care. You are proving her to be right, acting like a child,'

'Well, I am sixteen, Dad. Technically, I'm still a child, so I'm only acting how I should be!'

Leon rubs his head.

'The day you find your mate, I'll worry about him. That's for sure,' Leon says.

'Dad! How can you say that? You're just as bad as the old crone, you know!'

Leon holds his hand up to silence May.

'Shh, you hear that?'

May stops her tantrum, and we all listen.

'What do you hear, Dad?' May whispers.

'I hear silence, and that's all I want to hear. Now be quiet so we can focus on finding your sister,'

Again, I must cover my mouth with my hand to contain my laugh. May turns and glares at me. I gulp and swallow my laughter but keep the smirk on my face.

Mabel has a grin as wide as the Nile River plastered on her face.

We follow Mabel quietly until she stops in front of a dark cave.

'The other cave looked much more welcoming than this one,' May pouts.

'You wouldn't last five minutes in that cave, dear. Looks can be deceiving. This one here may be dark and gloomy, but it leads to the ruthless rogue pack,' Mabel says.

Leon shifts into his wolf to see better. I want to shift too, but it will take too long, and the rogues will hear my yells of pain, which will give us away.

Mabel flicks a stick, and a tiny ball of light appears like a flame. She hands it to me, then flicks her finger against the tip of another stick and hands it to May.

'How did you do that?' May says in amazement.

I look at Mabel.

'You're a witch?' I say.

'Shh,' she smiles, 'This way,' she waves.

We follow her through the shallow, murky water.

I can hear the sounds of frogs and rats. May is shaking like a leaf at the number of cobwebs and spiders we pass. The one cave now has three different tunnels. We stop and stare at them.

'Which one is the right way?' I ask Mabel.

'Always keep to the left on the way in and keep to the right on the way out.' She says.

I turn to thank her as she vanishes into the shadows.

'How did she disappear like that?' May asks.

'Magic,' I shrug.

'So, which way do we go?'

'Left, let's go.'

CHAPTER 27

We trudge down the left tunnel, holding our magically lit sticks in the air that illuminates the cave. Leon, still in wolf form, grabs a rat and eats it.

'So gross, Dad!' May says.

Leon ignores her and finishes his meal. We continue through the tunnel to find another two tunnels.

'We go left,' I say before May even asks.

The tunnel becomes smaller. I have to bend my head down to fit. After hours of being in here, we finally see the light at the end of the tunnel.

We can hear yelling in the distance and approach with caution. Peeking our heads out, it is almost nightfall. I touch the end of the lit stick. It's not hot, so I tuck it into my pocket to hide the glow. May does the same. We follow the sound of people yelling. There are some thick bushes nearby. I signal for Leon and May to follow me. I crawl into the bushes and inspect the commotion.

A large circle of stones with sticks and branches in the middle are waiting to be set alight. An oversized stone chair carved out of what had once been a boulder was now in its place. It has a throne-like look to it.

There is a she-wolf with her hands tied together with rope. A rogue approaches her from behind and kicks her down to the ground.

'Hurry and fetch the wine, wench!' He yells.

A dozen rogues appear exiting from another cave nearby. The she-wolf, with her hands tied, runs into the cave. After a few minutes, she leaves the cave with a jug and places it by the stone chair. Another she-wolf exits the cave carrying a pitcher. She looks to be around my mum's age. As the moon rises, more rogues appear and gather around the circle of stones.

The rogues chant, 'Moss, Moss, Moss!' Finally, he enters the ceremony, chest out, with a pompous look as if he is ultimate and superior to all.

230

'I can't see Nina anywhere,' I say.

'I can't see her either,' May says.

Moss approaches the stone throne and sits. He takes a chalice from the ground and looks at the poor girl on the ground who holds a jug of wine.

'Hurry and fill my damn cup. You're probably the most useless slave yet,'

'Yes, Alpha, Sorry Alpha,' the girl says, kneeling and filling his chalice.

'Is everyone ready for my wolf ceremony?' He yells.

'Yes!' Everyone cheers.

'Someone, bring out our future Luna to start this celebration!' Moss says.

They drag Nina out of the cave. Her hands are tied, and she is unkempt, with a few scrapes and bruises on her lower legs and knees. They have kept her in a dirty cell all this time.

My eyes are black with rage. My wolf wants to kill every rogue celebrating. Pain surges through my body as I'm about to yell at my pain. May covers my mouth with her hand tightly.

'Don't you dare make a sound,' she warns.

I swallow my pain and focus on controlling my wolf. Once I'm calm, I watch as someone forcibly places Nina on the ground on the other side of the stone throne.

The slave and Nina give each other a sympathetic look.

'Smile, Nina, it's my wolf ceremony. At least pretend to be happy,' Moss says.

Nina spits at his feet.

'I'll smile when I turn your wolf ceremony into your wolf's funeral,' she yells.

'If you weren't my chosen mate, I would make you receive ten lashes. Instead, I'll give your punishment to Gianna for your insolence,'

Gianna must be a slave.

'No, you can't punish her. Leave her alone. Punish me instead,' Nina cries.

Moss nods for two rogues to take Gianna to a post and loops her tied hands over it. Nina runs to Gianna and hugs her tight.

'No, get away from her!' Nina screams.

Another rogue approaches and drags Nina away back towards Moss.

'We need to do something. We can't just sit back and watch,' I say to May.

'They outnumber us. What do we do?' May asks.

Moss grabs Nina's wrist. Nina tries to fight him off. Moss laughs, pulls Nina onto his lap, and holds her arms down. He is going to force Nina to watch Gianna receive ten lashes.

My eyes are black again. I yell in pain as the rogue gives Gianna her first lash.

She screams, but they stop the lashing and turn towards my yells of pain.

'This isn't good. They know we are here,' May says.

'I'm going to shift. I can't control my wolf,' I tell her.

'Dad and I will distract them for as long as we can while you shift,'

I nod and yell as a few bones snap.

The stick in May's pocket glows brighter. We all stare at it in awe as rogues approach.

'I wonder?' May says as she pulls it out and holds it up. 'The spells we read in the book of spells and hexes, Magnus!' She exclaims.

I'm confused. I give May a strange look before another bone breaks.

May steps out from the bushes, holds the stick high, and yells 'Tumultuous Volley!'

Thunder erupts, and dark clouds appear and swirl around high above the rogues.

Tumultuous Volley is one of the spells I read in that book. It summons a storm and strikes enemies down with lightning.

The rogues pause and look up at the storm brewing above them. Then, one by one, lightning strikes them down. She-wolves scream and scatter.

Moss and the others look on with horror.

'May!' Nina screams.

The rogues spread out to avoid the storm and run towards May.

'Oh no, M-Magnus, what was the flame spell?'

'Inferno Flamo,' I yell.

'Inferno Flamo,' she repeats loudly.

A ball of flame appears. May aims and flings it towards a rogue, and then another ball of flame appears. She knocks down as many rogues as she can as they run towards the creek to put the flames out.

I've finally shifted. I let out a fierce howl. Leon stays by my side as we attack the rogues. We lunge and bite into them and fling their bodies away. An elderly she-wolf comes out of the cave with a furious look on her face. The rogues that can shift into a wolf do so and run towards Leon and me.

We are getting closer to Moss. He drags Nina towards the old lady and the other woman. As they take Nina's wrists, he falls to the ground and yells as his bones snap. His first shift has begun.

Within a couple of minutes, he shifted. His wolf is large and brown with a grey tail and grey ears. Not a handsome wolf at all. I must be twice his size as well.

He lets out a terrible howl, not the least bit intimidating, and runs towards Leon and me fighting his rogues. Moss lunges at Leon and bites his leg. Leon whimpers and tries to fight off another rogue already attacking him. I lunge at Moss and knock him over with ease. Balls of flame are shooting past us, and thick fog appears everywhere as May yells.

'Tremendous Nebulus!'

The only person I can see is Moss, snarling and snapping his teeth at me. I can hear Nina yelling my name.

'Magnus!'

Moss lunges at me. I snap my teeth over his front leg, breaking it. He lets out a howl of pain and snarls back at me. Before he makes his next move, I lunge, knocking him onto his back. I press my front paws on his chest to keep him down and rip ferociously into his neck. He falls limp as a puddle of blood forms on his torn open neck. As the fog dissipates, the woman around my mother's age lets out a horrific scream and runs towards Moss's dead body.

'No! Not my son. He can't be dead!' She screams, cradling his head. I take a few steps back. She looks up at me with a fierce stare.

'You, you will pay for this. I should have killed your mother long ago, and now I will kill you too!'

CHAPTER 28

The older woman grabs the younger woman's shoulder but stares at me.

'It's over for now, but this won't be the last you see of us,' she hisses.

I growl and step towards them. May places her hand on my back.

'No, let them go. We need to find Nina. We can worry about them later,' May says as the two women quickly shift and run away. I shift back and yell in pain. After a few minutes, I'm in my human form. Leon shifts back as well.

'Nina!' I cry out.

There are dead bodies everywhere. Gianna is sobbing. May approaches Gianna and unties her from the post and the rope from her wrists.

I hear a moan and a mumble and run towards the sound. Pushing a couple of bodies aside, I find Nina.

'Nina, I'm here. You're safe now,' I say, untying her wrists. She squints her eyes, letting them adjust. The look of relief shows on her face. Nina sits up, lunges into my lap, wraps her arms around my neck, and cries into my chest.

'You came for me. You found me,'

'Of course, we came for you, Nina. I would search the ends of the Earth for you,'

She cries even louder and holds me tighter.

'I thought I'd never see you again,'

Leon approaches.

'Dad!' Nina stands up and runs into his arms.

'My baby girl, I was so worried,'

Nina looks over to May, looking at the whiplash on Gianna's back.

'May, Gianna,' she says, releasing herself from Leon.

May and Nina hug each other.

'I thought you hated me?' May says.

'Although you have been a horrible sister to me all my life, I'm glad you're here.'

Nina checks Gianna's back, 'It's already healing,' she says.

'I've had my wolf for a month now, which means I heal quickly,' Gianna says.

'Are you okay?' I ask Gianna.

'I will be now that Moss and his rogues are dead,' she says.

'How long have you been captive here for?' I ask.

'Over a year... I think anyway. The rogues would never tell me what day or month it was,'

'What pack did they take you from?'

'I was never in a pack. I lived in an orphanage, and they kicked me and anyone else who turned sixteen that year. I spent a year living on the streets until one night, when I was about to fall asleep, a man approached me, sniffing the air. He smiled at me, said, "She-wolf," and took me away to join them. They wanted me to join them for breeding purposes. I tried to escape many times. I didn't want to be there. I was better off in the streets than here,' she frowns.

'Gianna, we would love you to join our pack, a real pack where you will have freedom and friendships?' I offer.

'You would want me to come with you?' She says with a raised eyebrow.

'Yes, we would,'

She looks at Nina, who smiles and nods her head yes at Gianna.

Gianna cries and hugs Nina.

'If it's not too much trouble, I would love to come with you all,'

'Well, Gianna,' May smiles, 'We must introduce ourselves. I'm Nina's younger sister May, and this is our father, Leon and our future Alpha, Magnus,'

'I'm so happy to meet you all,' she smiles.

Nina takes a step back in thought.

'Um, May, how did you summon a storm, fireballs, and fog?'

'Well, you see. We came across a witch who led us here. She gave Magnus and me a stick and made it light up like a torch. When we were in trouble, the wand illuminated more, and I had the sudden urge to say a spell out loud from the book of spells and hexes Magnus showed us. Then I realised they weren't just sticks but wands. So, I shouted one spell out loud, and it worked.'

'But only witches can use wands, so how is this possible?' Leon asks.

I take the wand from my pocket, whirl it around, and point it at a shrub, 'Inferno Flamo,' I say, and we watch as nothing happens.

I pass the wand to Gianna, 'Inferno Flamo?' She says. Again, nothing happens.

'Why does it only work for May?' I ask.

Nina takes the wand, 'Inferno Flamo,' she says, and a gigantic ball of flame appears and flies fiercely through the air over a mountain. We hear the impact in the distance, causing a touch of smoke to rise into the sky.

Everyone has shocked faces as we all turn to stare at Nina.

'Umm, oops, a daisy?'

'Oops, a daisy?' May says. 'You just summoned a ball of flame the size of a house and made it fly a kilometre away! And all you can say is, oops, a daisy?'

'Well, gee-whiz May, ever think I might be just as shocked as you all are with what I did? What do you expect me to say?'

'I just want to know why you girls can use wands? This is not normal for a wolf to wield magic,' Leon says, confused.

'Maybe it's just temporary?' I suggest.

'It will take us a week to get back to Shadow Crest. This is very dangerous. We mustn't mention this magic to anyone in the pack other than Alpha Ryker and Our Luna Astrid. Got it?'

We all nod in agreement and enter the cave to leave.

'Keep to the right.' I say as we reach two separate tunnels. Nina and May hold their wands up, illuminating the cave. We step out of the exit and into the woods. The only light we can see is from the wands lighting our path: Nina and May yawn.

'Let's make a fire and sleep here the night. We are all exhausted, and it must be around 2 am,' I say.

The girls sit down next to Leon, and I gather sticks and bundle them together.

'Inferno Flamo,' Nina says, pointing her wand at the bundle of sticks. A flame the size of my hand shoots from the wand to the stick, setting them alight. Leon and I give her a look.

'What?' She says, 'I may as well make the most of it while it lasts?' She shrugs.

I sit next to Nina on the end as she hovers her hands close to the fire, warming them up. She leans her head on my shoulder. I can feel her body shaking from the cold. I drape my arm over her shoulder to give her my body warmth.

As I wake up, I can feel something warm covering me. I open my eyes and see Nina asleep with her hand and head on my chest.

My hand strokes her arm, gently waking her. Her eyes flutter open, and we smile and sit up.

'Let's wake the others,' I say.

Nina nods and wakes Gianna and May up while I wake Leon up.

'I'm so thirsty,' Gianna says, stretching her arms out.

'We have bottles of water and snacks in the car. You can help yourself as soon as we are there,' I tell her.

'How far away is the car?'

'About an hour's walk,'

'Okay,' she smiles.

Nina and I walk side by side as the others walk ahead.

'What does it feel like to wield magic?' I ask her.

'Honestly, it feels amazing. It's a shame I won't be able to show it off back at Shadow Crest,' Nina laughs.

'Josie would think it's the best thing ever,' I say.

'Until I turn her into a frog,' Nina replies.

We both burst into laughter.

'Is that spell even in the book? I don't recall reading it in there,'

'No, but I will have to study the book further to learn all the spells I can cast,' she says.

'If my parents learn about the spellbook, they might take it away. It's all we have that could help us break your curse,'

'Then the book can remain a secret then.' She smiles.

CHAPTER 29

We arrive at the car.

'I'll mind-link Ryker and let him know we have Nina and are safe.'

I open the back passenger door—Gianna steps in, then Nina. May sits in the front. My heart rate increases as I get to sit next to Nina. I unzip the bag at my feet and pass out a bottle of water to everyone. Nina and Gianna scull the water down before I hand them snacks. They moan as they eat the food, especially Gianna. She eats a packet of chips, a muesli bar and three chocolate bars.

'This is so good. I've never had food like this before, not even when I was at the orphanage,' Gianna says with her mouth full of food.

'We will get you a proper meal when we reach the next town,' Leon says to her while adjusting the rear-view mirror.

As we reach the town, we park outside the diner. We raced inside, causing a lot of attention from the diners and staff. We sit at the nearest table and wave the waitress over. She takes the pen behind her ear and the notepad from her pocket.

'What would you like to order, please?' She smiles.

'I'll have pancakes with syrup and ice cream on top, a cherry pie, fries, bacon, and eggs on toast, and a milkshake,' Nina blurts out.

We all look at her, then at the waitress, and all say.

'I'll have the same,'

'Very well then,' the waitress says.

We eat like it's our last supper and shuffle back to the car.

'We can get a motel in this town, or if we get back on the road, we can reach the next town by nightfall?'

'I think the sooner we arrive home, the better, so let's get back on the road and get to the next town,'

'As long as I get a bath today, I don't care,' Nina says, looking down at her dirty arms and legs.

We reach the next town just at nightfall and enter the motel. I pay for two rooms next to each other. They both have a single bed and a double in each room, with a bathroom attached to each room.

'May, are you able to see if you can find some clean clothes for Nina and Gianna while they freshen up?'

'I'll see what I can do,' May says, leaving the motel room.

'You girls can take this room, and Leon and I will be in the room next door. Nina, while Gianna baths in your bathroom, you can come and use ours?'

'Sure, that would be great.'

Gianna walks into the bathroom and locks the door behind her while Nina and I walk into my room. I open the bathroom door and close it behind her.

'I'm going to get us some takeaway food from up the road. I'll be back soon.' Leon says.

The sound of water fills the tub while I lie on my bed in silence.

'Magnus?' Nina calls.

'Yeah?' I stand up and walk to the bathroom door, 'Is everything okay?'

'Yeah, um, I just want to make sure I wasn't alone,'

'You're not alone, and you'll never be alone again,' I say, with my head leaning against the bathroom door.

'Do you promise?' She asks after a moment of silence.

I open the door and sit next to the tub on the floor.

The bubbles are up to her neck. She most likely poured an entire bottle into the bath. I smile to myself, thinking of the washing machine incident.

We turn our heads to face each other.

'I'm scared, Magnus. Moss's mum is going to come after us. I just know it,'

'I won't let her harm you,'

'But what if she finds a way?'

'Mark my word, Nina. I will kill her before she lays a finger on you again,'

'I wish if it was something else you could mark,' she whispers and stares sadly into my eyes.

Just as I have powerful feelings for Nina, she has practically just confessed her feelings to me. Our faces lean in slowly, and our lips brush as we are about to kiss. Then she quickly sits back, taking in a deep breath.

'Magnus, we can't do this. We aren't mates. It would be wrong of us. It's forbidden for us to consider being together.'

I want to hold her, kiss her, make love, and never let her go. But seeing her so sad like this is breaking my heart.

I reach my hand out to caress her cheek.

'Magnus, please, don't. I need you to stop. I need you to go,'

'But...'

'Go!'

I stand up and immediately leave the bathroom. As soon as I shut the door, I hear Nina burst into tears. I'm overwhelmed and confused; I need some air. Leaving the room, I bump into May, causing her to drop the clothes she carries. I don't stop to help pick up the clothes. Instead, I speed walk out of the motel as she yells after me.

'Magnus, is everything ok?' I ignore her.

Running up a hill, I sit on top and stare at the moon.

'What's wrong with me? Why do I have feelings for Nina when she isn't my mate? Why does it have to be forbidden to have a chosen mate instead of a fated mate?' I remain staring at the moon for hours.

I return to the motel to find a frantic Leon.

'Where have you been?' He says and takes in my morbid-looking face.

'What happened, Magnus? You look worse than Nina does,' he frowns.

I don't answer and walk into our room, kicking my shoes off, pulling my shirt over my head, and tossing it aside. I climb into the closest bed, cover myself, including my face, with the covers, and sleep.

That morning Leon wakes me up.

'I know you have had little sleep, Magnus, but we need to go so we can get through a few towns,'

Leon passes me my shirt. I quickly shower, get dressed, and walk straight to the car. May is already in the front passenger's seat, which I was hoping to take. Gianna is in the back seat, and Leon is in the driver's seat. I notice Nina isn't in the car yet. I open the back passenger door, sit beside Gianna, and wait for Nina.

'Is everything okay, Magnus? You seemed a bit upset last night. I noticed Nina was upset, too. Did you two have a fight or something?' May asks.

I shrug my shoulders and sit back. Nina exits the motel wearing clean track pants and a plain shirt.

'The motel had a lost and found compartment with lots of clothes. The manager told me to help myself,' May says.

I notice Gianna is wearing clean overalls and a shirt, too. Nina steps into the car.

'Let's go.' She murmurs.

After a few hours of driving, we stop for a toilet break and for lunch.

Sitting at the table eating, everyone speaks, except for Nina and me. We sit as far away from each other as possible. It was evident to everyone something was up, but they also knew not to get involved and say anything.

'How much longer until we get to Shadow Crest?' Gianna asks.

'At this rate, two more nights. The night before Nina's wolf ceremony, which the Alpha and Luna are already organising,' Leon says.

Nina looks even sadder now that Leon mentioned her wolf ceremony. She abruptly stands up, walks away from the table, and towards the car.

'I guess that's our cue to get back on the road then?' May says.

The silent drive is almost deafening. I can tell May is struggling not to say anything.

It's nightfall, and we arrive at a motel. Unfortunately, they only have one room available with two double beds.

'Who is going to sleep on the floor?' May asks.

'I'll sleep in the car. You all go in,' I say.

'Are you sure? Are you okay?' May asks.

No, I'm not. I want to be by Nina's side, even if it means sleeping on the floor. I'm upset Nina rejected me and that it's forbidden for us to be together, but I don't tell May that.

'Yes, I'm sure.' I grizzle and walk back to the car.

No matter how hard I tried, I couldn't sleep, and I couldn't stop thinking about Nina. I felt like it was almost killing me. The thought of never being with Nina is almost too much to bear.

CHAPTER 30

As soon as the sun rose, Leon came to check on me.

'You look worse every time I see you, Magnus,' he

frowns.

'Are the girls ready to go? I want to get out of here,' I

say, ignoring his observation.

'Yeah, I'll tell them to hurry it up,'

'Good.' I say and sit in the front passenger's seat.

Minutes later, the girls climb in the back, talking to one

another as I stare out the front window. I pull the visor in

front of me down and slide the panel across, exposing the

small mirror. Leon wasn't wrong when he commented

about my appearance. The bags under my eyes have only

become more prominent and darker. I notice May give

Nina a look and gesture her head at me. She was hinting to

Nina to say something to me. Nina glares at May, shakes her head no, and looks out the window, avoiding me.

Leon enters the driver's seat and puts the radio on to break the silence.

May sings along to half the songs throughout the day. We stop for petrol, and Leon buys snacks for everyone while we are there. The girls tell Leon they are going to the lady's room. Leon offers me some snacks, but I refuse. I haven't eaten much since Nina told me to go.

We all get back to the car and continue the drive.

'One more night at a motel, and we should arrive at Shadow crest mid-morning tomorrow.' Leon says.

The girls are thrilled and excited. I look forward to seeing Flint, Josie, and my parents. I wonder how Zak and Pipsqueak are going? He is so lucky to have found his mate straight away. I've been through dozens of towns searching for Nina with no traces of a mate along the way. I would have smelt her scent if she was in the towns or villages. My inner wolf would have forced me to follow her scent.

'My wolf is aching to get out for a run,' Gianna says.

'Mine too, but I've been trying to hold it off for as long as possible. We can shift and go for a quick run when we reach a rural area,' Leon says.

'That would be great.'

Half an hour goes by, and Leon pulls over by some fields. He shifts behind the car and runs through the field. Gianna shifts and follows him on the run.

'I can't wait until I can shift,' May says, watching them.

'You only have a couple more years to wait, and at least you can cast magic in the meantime,' Nina says.

'That's true. Let's go practice while they are having their run.'

Nina nods and exits the car. I'm the only one left in the vehicle. I can't shift without it causing unbearable pain to join the others, and Nina doesn't want me near her. I feel like an outsider and that I don't belong here. My inner wolf whines and whimpers, but I ignore him. He doesn't like my thoughts, but I don't care.

'What was the spell to cast water?' May asks Nina.

'I think it was aqua something?'

'Yes, that's right,' I watch May swirl her wand around 'Aqua beads!' Nothing happens, 'Aqua shoot!' Again nothing, 'Aqua burst!'

I remember reading the spell. It's "Aqua bedew," but I decide not to say anything and keep watching instead.

Leon and Gianna return from their run.

'What are you girls doing?' Leon asks.

'Trying to summon and cast water,' May says nonchalantly.

'Girls, I don't know how I feel about you doing magic. Just because you can do something doesn't mean you should. You know magic is forbidden. Why do you think the last remaining few witches are in hiding? I want you girls to promise me no more magic until we have spoken to Alpha Ryker and our Luna?'

'Yes, Dad.' They both groan.

May and Nina begrudgingly get into the car, and we drive for the rest of the day with no more stops until we reach the last town for the day.

Leon pays for two rooms again. One for the girls and one for us. Leon has a shower as I flick through the channels on TV. The girls are giggling and carrying on in the next room. Frustrated with the TV, I turn it off, remove my shoes, and climb into bed. I'll be happy to be home tomorrow, and everything can return to normal. I'll finish the last few weeks of school and graduate, then mum and dad will probably tell me to hurry and find my mate. Then I can take over and become the next Alpha.

I sigh at the thought. If only it were going to be that easy.

The girls have become quiet. They have probably gone to bed. I switch the bedside lamp off and go to sleep.

As soon as I wake, I have my shower and dress. Leon hands me a plate with an egg and lettuce sandwich.

'You need to eat something, Magnus,'

I don't argue with him. Instead, I accept the plate and eat the sandwich.

'Can you knock on the girl's door and tell them to meet us in the car?' Leon says.

'Sure,' I sigh.

I leave our room and knock on the door. Nina answers, and we stare at each other in silence.

'Your dad wanted me to tell you, girls, we are ready to get going,'

'Oh, okay.' Nina says and shuts the door.

Feeling defeated, I hop into the front passenger side of the car. Leon is already in the car. After twenty minutes, the girls all climb into the back seat.

After hours of driving, we pass the Welcome to Shadow Crest sign. As Leon parks the car, I jump out and run inside the packhouse. My mum is the first one I see. I wrap my arms around her tiny body and lift her off the ground-hugging her tight.

'Magnus, my boy. I missed you so much,' she cries.

'I missed you too, Mum.' I say and wipe her tears from her face.

Josie and Flint come running down the stairs. Josie flies into my chest first. I hug her tightly, and then Flint and I hug each other.

Leon, Nina, May, and Gianna enter the packhouse. Mum hugs Nina.

'I'm so glad you are back home,'

'Me too, Luna,'

'Nina?' Amelia yells, running out of the kitchen. 'Nina!' She wraps her arms around her and kisses her face a hundred times.

'I was so worried,'

'Mum, I'm okay now,'

My Dad enters and pulls me in for a hug.

Gianna stands there awkwardly.

'Mum, Dad, this is Gianna. She was forced to be a slave in Moss's pack,' Astrid and Amelia gasp.

'Is it okay if she joins our pack?'

'Of course, it's okay. You poor thing,' Astrid says and pulls her in for a hug.

'Gianna can have the spare room next to Nina's room until she finds her mate,' Ryker says.

'Thank you for letting me stay,' Gianna says.

'I'll show you to your room,' May says and takes her hand.

'You must all be hungry. Let's have lunch, and you can tell us everything,' Astrid says.

Leon explains how we met Mabel and how she led us to Moss's pack.

'Magnus was trying to fight his wolf from shifting. They heard his cries of pain, and that's when May summoned a storm, balls of fire and fog saving us all.' Leon says, then nervously laughs.

Astrid, Ryker, Josie, and Flint burst into laughter. Except for Amelia, whose face suddenly becomes pale.

'Good one, Leon, so continue. Tell us what really happened,' Ryker says.

Leon and I give each other a nervous look. Nina won't even look up from the table and fiddles nervously with her fingers.

'Well, Alpha… that's what actually happened,' Leon says.

The room grows silent as they all stare at Leon.

'It's true, Dad. Nina can cast magic from the wands as well,' I say.

'That's impossible. May and Nina are wolves, not witches,' he says.

Nina gives me a worried look.

'It's okay, Nina, show them,' I say.

Nina hesitantly nods and stands up.

She pulls the wand from her back pocket and swirls it around.

'Aqua...'

'Bedew,' I whisper.

Nina gives me a small smile.

'Aqua Bedew.' She says, and a small swirl of water appears. Nina directs it into a cup on the table.

It's so quiet that I can hear everyone's heart rate rapidly increase.

CHAPTER 31

'This is impossible,' Ryker says, standing up, 'This can't be happening? Magic has been long gone and forbidden for many years. We only discovered that a few witches still exist when you had that fever, Magnus,'

Astrid clears her throat, 'Nina, you and your sister, cannot experiment with this. You are already in danger due to your curse affecting Magnus, and now to learn you can cast magic. It will cause mass panic. Everyone will hunt you and May down. The only way to keep you both safe is for either of you not to cast magic,' she says.

I know how much being able to cast spells has meant to Nina. She is trying hard to hold back tears and hide her feelings from everyone.

'We need to figure out how this is even possible,' Ryker says.

We all look at Leon and Amelia. Leon shrugs his shoulders, 'I'm in just as much shock as you all are. I swear I do not know,' he says, then looks at Amelia, who has the look of guilt written all over her face. 'Amelia?' Leon says.

'Well, you see. There is something I haven't told anyone before. I didn't see the point until now,' Amelia takes a deep breath, 'My grandma was a witch,'

'What?' Everyone says in shock.

'My grandfather was a wolf. It turned out my grandmother was a witch. They knew it wasn't right. It was unheard of, a witch and a wolf being fated mates. They tried hard to stay away from each other but found it impossible. My mother and another child were born to them. Neither could wield magic, but both were able to shift into wolves at eighteen. My mother had me, and I was never able to wield magic. We all figured the wolf gene must have been stronger, and having two generations without magic thought it would never happen to future generations. Now it seems it happened… two generations later. Nina and May are half-witch, half-wolf,'

We all look at one another, taking it all in.

'None of this information is to leave this room. Nina, I will leave it to you to tell May she is to no longer cast magic,' Ryker says.

Nina stands up and runs up the stairs without saying a word. I know she is upset.

'There's something else you and Mum need to know, Dad,' I say.

'What!'

'Moss… is dead. I killed him. He shifted and came at me, intending to kill me. He would have taken Nina back,'

'You did what you had to do to protect our pack members. I'm sure the wolf council will understand,'

'That's not all. His mother was there she said we would pay for this. That she should have killed my mother long ago and that she will kill me too. You must know who she is?'

Astrid and Ryker give each other a worried look.

'Did you see her wolf? Any of their wolves? What colour were they?' Astrid asks.

'Moss's wolf was brown with grey ears and a grey tail, and when his mother shifted, she was small, brown and scruffy with a grey patch on her side,'

'Vanessa!' Astrid and Ryker say together in shock.

Ryker looks at Leon.

'Have double the warriors at each post in case Vanessa tries to attack us,'

'I don't think Vanessa would be capable of much harm on her own, though?' I say.

'Don't underestimate her son. Knowing Vanessa, she will have more rogues somewhere,' Astrid says.

I leave the table and go up to my room. May's bedroom door is ajar. I hear Nina informing May that they are both banned from using magic.

'This is so unfair!' May says.

I continue to my room and close the door. I fall backwards onto my bed and stare up at the roof.

After a while, there was a knock at my door. It's May.

'Um, hey, Nina is wondering if she could borrow the spellbook from you, please?'

'She knows you are both banned from casting magic and spells. So I can't loan either of you the book. Even I shouldn't have the book,'

'Please, Magnus, let her borrow it just for tonight?'

I sigh, walk over to my school bag, unzip it, and take the spellbook out.

'I will give it to her myself,'

'Okay,' she smiles and follows me.

I stop and face May.

'Alone...' I say.

'Oh... I'll just be going to my room then,' she says, annoyed.

I knock on Nina's door. It surprised her to see me, but she saw I held the book in my arms.

'Come in,' she says, stepping aside.

I hand her the book, but I don't let go, 'Promise me you won't get caught casting magic?'

'I'll try my best not to get caught,'

'That's not a promise, Nina.'

'I suggest you study as much as you can tonight from the book because I'm only letting you borrow it for tonight,'

'One night?' She protests.

'I'm not risking you being exiled or hunted down, Nina. However, if you need to study the book in the future, we will do it together so I can at least keep a watch out for anyone snooping around,'

Nina looks at the spellbook in thought and nods.

'Deal,'

'Tomorrow is your wolf ceremony, and it will be a busy day. So read what you can now and get some sleep. You will need all the energy you can get for your first shift tomorrow night.' I tell her.

She walks me to her door and closes it behind me. My wolf wants to shift and go for a run. He is very restless all night. I struggle to get any sleep. Everyone is having breakfast. I'm surprised to see Pipsqueak at the table but then remember she is Zak's mate, so it's only natural she lives in the packhouse with him now. We give each other a smile and a wave. Zak enters the dining room with a growl and pulls Pipsqueak from her chair.

'Mine,' he growls, glaring at me.

'Gee, is it normal for the mate bond to make you so possessive?' I ask.

'Yup,' Mia laughs.

'The mate bond is a funny thing to experience,' Seth smiles at Mia.

'It's the most magical feeling,' Astrid says, 'It's like static electricity when you touch each other. You can't stop thinking about your mate and yearn to be with them every second of the day. You feel broken and empty whenever you are apart. And let's not forget the mind-blowing sex you have,' Astrid laughs.

'Mum!' I growl.

Almost everyone at the table is blushing.

'What? It's only natural, dear,' she shrugs.

Amelia clears her throat, 'Nina will get her wolf tonight. I'm so excited,'

'Yeah, exciting,' Nina mumbles.

'Let's hope there is no drama this time, unlike Zak's wolf ceremony where Nina had been kidnapped,' Astrid says with a nervous laugh. Nina leaves the table as soon as she finishes breakfast. She runs upstairs and runs back down, now wearing a backpack.

'I'll be back in time for the ceremony,' she yells.

'Okay, sweetheart,' Leon says.

I decide to sneak out and follow her. She runs to the lake and pulls the spell book out.

'Aqua Bedew,' she says, twirling her wand. I watch as all the water comes together like a tornado. Then, all the water from the lake is gone and swirls up in the air.

'Cool,' I say, standing behind her. She flinches in fright, and the lake's water drops like a giant blob. The impact causes water to splash onto us.

She glares at me, drenched in water.

CHAPTER 32

'You scared me, Magnus! Don't sneak up on me like that again,'

'Sorry,' I say, ringing my shirt out.

Nina moves over to a dry area on the grass. I sit opposite her.

'What are you doing, Magnus?'

'Monitoring you, so you don't get caught,'

'I will not get caught, Magnus,'

'What spell are you going to try now?' I say, changing the subject.

'There is one here called The Blinking Spell, which says to focus on an area you can see in the distance, wave your wand, and say Skedaddle Dash. This will port you to that area. This spell can make you blink or teleport up to a one thousand metre radius at a time,'

'Think of how quickly you can get to school with that spell?' I laugh.

Nina rolls her eyes and stands up, walking roughly five metres away from me and looking past me into the distance.

'Okay, here goes nothing,' she says, waving her wand. 'Skedaddle Dash!'

She disappears for a split second. I suddenly feel a weight on my lap. I look down to see Nina blushing as I hold her like a baby in my arms.

I burst into laughter, 'I like this spell a lot,'

She shoves my chest and crawls out of my lap.

'That's not what was supposed to happen,' she growls.

'Well, you must have wanted to be in my arms, Nina. Remember, the magic only ports you to where you want to be within a one thousand metre radius,' I say, waving my index finger at her.

'You're so stupid, Magnus, don't think so highly of yourself,' she blushes, 'The spell didn't work properly, that's all,'

'I'm sure.' I smirk.

This time Nina faces away from me and stares at the other side of the lake. She twirls her wand 'Skedaddle Dash,' she yells. Her body blinks and instantly appears on the other side of the lake.

'I did it!'

'You did it!' I say.

'I can't believe I teleported that far!'

There is rustling from a nearby bush. I gesture my finger over my lip for Nina to be quiet. As I approach, a rabbit hops out of the bush. I'm instantly relieved after thinking someone has been watching us.

'It's just a rabbit, Nina laughs,'

Nina twirls her wand 'Skedaddle Dash,' she says and instantly appears in front of me, giggling.

'Tremendous Nebulus,' she says with a wave of her wand. A thick cloud of fog forms out of thin air in front of her. She twirls her wand around, spreading it over the lake.

I watch her spend most of the day practising spells from the book. She seems to be growing weary and tired.

'Nina, perhaps you should stop with the spells for now. They seem to drain all your energy?'

'No, I'm fine,' she says with a sway. I catch her before she falls. She is so tired she doesn't even try to fight me out of my arms. Instead, she snuggles up into my chest and falls asleep. I hold her tight and let her sleep. She has the cutest dimples and the sweetest smile on her face.

After a couple of hours, my eyes zone in onto the nape of her neck. My heart rate increases rapidly, and my face grows closer to her neck. My teeth protrude and lightly scrape the spot her mate is supposed to mark. I quickly flinch back and shake the urge to mark her out of my mind.

'What is wrong with me? She isn't even my mate, and I almost marked her,'

I have no choice but to wake her and move away from Nina before I end up doing something very foolish.

'Nina,' I say, rubbing her arm, 'Nina,'

'Mmm?' She mumbles.

'Time to wake up. Your ceremony begins soon,'

Nina rubs her eyes and blinks a few times. She crawls off me as soon as she realises she has been sleeping in my lap.

'Sorry,' she says.

'Don't be. You needed the sleep,'

'Thanks,' she smiles.

'Let's get home and get ready for your ceremony.'

She nods, and we walk back home.

She gives me the book of spells as we reach the top of the stairs.

'I'll see you shortly at the ceremony,' she says.

'You will.' I smile.

I place the book in my backpack and enter my room. I pick out a black suit, white shirt, and blue tie. As soon as I've showered and dressed, I head downstairs.

'Looking snazzy there, son,' Ryker says.

'Thanks. Is everyone ready for the ceremony?'

'We are just waiting on Nina.' Amelia says.

Moments later, Nina appears at the top of the staircase in a stunning silver sparkling dress with matching heels and diamond earrings. My heart wants to combust at her sheer beauty.

Flint slaps me hard on the back, knocking me out of my apparent trance.

'Try to be less obvious to your feelings, Magnus, if anyone sees you and Nina staring at each other like that when she isn't your mate. It will cause a lot of problems in the pack,'

'Less obvious of what feelings?' I ask.

'That you are in love with each other?'

I give him a weird look, 'You're seeing things, Flint. Nina and I care about each other as best friends, but we are not in love,'

'You keep telling yourself that.' He says with a hand on my shoulder.

I frown and move my shoulder from under his hand.

We all enter the ceremony hall and enjoy the banquet of food. We listen to many speeches. I notice Hank is at a table, glaring at me from across the room. He is probably angry that I got his Dad to agree on me choosing his daughter as my mate at my nineteenth instead of right away. I do my best to ignore him, but something seems off. The moon is now centred above the hall. It's time for Nina to step into the moonlight and shift. Her Dad, Leon, takes her hand and walks her to the centre of the hall, and places a kiss on her forehead. He walks away and takes his seat next to his mate, Amelia.

Minutes go by, and nothing happens. Nina gives me a worried look. I smile and nod my head to assure her not to worry. Hank is smiling while everyone else scratches their heads. Almost twenty minutes have gone by, and everyone whispers. Nina is holding her own, trying to remain calm and appear unaffected by nothing yet happening.

My Dad stands.

'Quiet everyone another round of drinks while we wait. I'm sure Nina's wolf will appear any moment now,' he assures everyone.

Another twenty minutes go by with no signs of Nina's wolf. Someone from a different pack stands up.

'If she doesn't have a wolf, that makes her a human.'

Everyone gasps and stares at Nina as she trembles and looks to me for help. I stand up and walk over to her and hold her hand.

Hank stands up and claps his hands. Everyone turns to stare at him.

'Bravo, Bravo.' He shouts. Everyone is confused.

Nina and I realise he is about to expose her curse.

I place my hands on her shoulders, 'Nina, what if this is the curse? That your wolf is dormant?'

'But that makes little sense of how it affects you, though?'

My face instantly pales as I revise a section of the spellbook in my head.

Anyone can also curse someone using their God's or Goddess's name. A powerful sign will occur, such as an earthquake, lightning strike, or a loud rumble from the sky if the god or goddess accepts your prayer, wish, or curse.

282

Then a flashback of when I was a child passes through my mind.

'Damn you, Nina, I wish if the Moon Goddess herself would curse you and not give you your wolf on your eighteenth birthday and remove your mate bond until the day I find my mate and fall in love,' I say out loud.

Then I remember the flash of lightning that suddenly hit the roof of the packhouse and the thunder that roared in the sky. It was the Moon Goddess accepting the curse!

'Nina… it affects me because I am the one who cursed you.' I say in realisation.

CHAPTER 33

Nina takes a step back, putting distance between us.

'Why would you do that to me? Why would you put a curse on me, Magnus?' She yells.

'She is cursed?' Someone yells.

Nina looks at me with tear-filled eyes and a look of anger and hurt in her eyes.

'Well, that's one less thing I don't have to tell.' Hank says.

Nina and I glare at him.

'Nina has a curse that affects your dear future, Alpha. He can't shift naturally without severe pain, as you all know, but you don't know it's because of her curse!' He shouts.

Everyone glares and points at Nina, mumbling angrily to each other.

'No, leave her alone! It's not her fault,' I say, pulling Nina behind my back.

'You're wrong, Magnus!' Hank shouts and turns to face the crowd, 'I have the proof that Nina is not what she seems. She has no wolf because she is a witch and cursed your future Alpha.' He holds a remote up, pressing a button. The projection screen shows a video of Nina and me and the lake earlier today. Nina is casting spells.

There is a sudden uproar of pack members and people from other packs yelling, 'Witch!', 'She cursed Magnus,' 'What if she has cursed others?'

Nina clings tightly to the back of my suit jacket.

My dad stands up and walks in front of us with my mother.

'Please, everyone. You must all calm down and take your seats. Nina is not a danger to anyone,' he says.

'See, she has even cursed your Alpha to protect her,' Hank yells.

'Nina would never,' Astrid shouts.

'I suppose they haven't told you either that their son Magnus killed Moss?'

'What?' Everyone says.

'He kidnapped Nina. He wanted to kill me,' I explain.

'Lies! I have a witness here who witnessed the brutal murder of her son.' He says, gesturing for someone to come forward.

A hooded figure steps out from the shadows, stands next to Hank, and pulls her hood down.

'Vanessa!' My parents scowl.

'It's true. Magnus murdered my son after Nina bewitched him. She made him fall in love with her. She willingly came to our pack, pretending we had kidnapped her. Magnus went straight for my son, who was under a spell and ripped him to pieces. And now I will seek my revenge!' She yells.

The hall becomes swarmed with hooded figures. Everyone yells and screams. The rogues remove their cloaks, shift into wolves, and attack my pack.

Astrid, Ryker, Leon, Seth, Mia, and Amelia instantly shift and fight off the rogues. I step back, keeping Nina safe behind me. We watch as my mother's wolf goes straight for Vanessa. Astrid lunges at Vanessa. They bite each other and roll, snapping and snarling. I have never seen my mother so vicious and put up such a fight with pure intent to kill. They fight to the death, one that was due many years ago. Astrid whimpers as Vanessa rips a chunk of flesh from her side. Astrid uses her weight to pin Vanessa down and bites into Vanessa's neck the same way I bit into Moss's. Blood pools at her neck as her legs flinch a few times before she becomes limp. Astrid lets out a howl of triumph. She has won the fight against her greatest enemy.

She spots Alice and runs towards her. Alice being old, my mother kills her within seconds. The rogues don't stop fighting, even though Vanessa is dead. Five of them creep towards Nina and me.

'Magnus, they're going to kill us?' Nina says.

'Use your wand. I need you to teleport out of here,'

Nina nods and pulls her wand out.

She grabs my arm. I look down at her as she says, 'Skedaddle Dash!'

We disappear together and reappear in the packhouse at the top of the stairs.

'Wait, you could port me too?'

'I figured it was worth a try,' she says, marching towards my room.

'Wait, where are you going?'

'I'm leaving, Magnus. I need to take the spellbook with me,' she says, searching through my room.

'Wait, what do you mean you're leaving?'

'Even if your parents beat the rogues, the pack will want to hunt me down anyway because, in case you have forgotten, they think I have cursed you when it's you who has cursed me,' she retorts.

'I won't let them hurt you. I'll explain everything. That it's all my fault,'

'Yeah, because you explaining it was going down well in the ceremony hall?' She says sarcastically, 'How do you suppose you will stop our pack and many others from hurting me when you can't even shift into a wolf quickly enough to save me?'

I walk over to my backpack, put it on, and take Nina's hand.

'What are you doing? Let me go,'

I stop and face her.

289

'I'm going with you,'

'What?'

'I'm leaving Shadow Crest. I'm going with you until I break the curse. That way, we can return, and no one will have a reason to harm you,'

'But they know I'm a witch,'

'And you can threaten to turn them into a frog if they even try to harm you,' I smile.

Nina is trying to stay angry at me. I watch her lips slightly curl up as she contains a laugh and nods and holds my arm and waves her wand. 'Skedaddle Dash, Skedaddle Dash, Skedaddle Dash,' she says a few times. We appear a thousand metres ahead with a blink of an eye, then another thousand metres. The blinking continues until we are at least a kilometre from Shadow Crest. As we come to a stop and are no longer teleporting, my stomach churns, and nausea takes over. I vomit profusely into the bushes. After ten minutes of vomiting, I turn and face an unimpressed Nina with her arms crossed.

'You have a lot of explaining to do, Magnus, such as why you cursed me, how you caused it and how you will break it?'

'Do you remember the day when we were kids, and you tricked me into standing near the floodgates by the dam, and I got washed away?'

'Yeah,' she laughs.

'That night, after mum told me to go bath, I went upstairs to my room and ran the bath. I was still soaking wet, and my clothes clung to my body. I slipped over and remained on the floor in anger. Then I stared out the window at the sky and yelled these words at the moon.

Damn you, Nina, I wish the Moon Goddess herself would curse you and not give you your wolf on your eighteenth birthday and remove your mate bond until the day I find my mate and I fall in love. After I said that, a flash of lightning suddenly hit the roof of the packhouse, and thunder roared in the sky. I wondered if it was a sign from the Moon Goddess but didn't think it was possible. I never thought about that moment until tonight when you didn't shift. Then I remembered this part in the spellbook,'

291

I pull the spell book out, open it, and point to the paragraph where it says.

Anyone can also curse someone using their God's or Goddess's name. A powerful sign will occur, such as an earthquake, lightning strike, or a loud rumble from the sky if the God or Goddess accepts your prayer, wish, or curse.

'That was when I realised it was me who had cursed you. I'm so sorry, Nina, I am truly sorry,' I say as tears drip down her face. She steps back, glaring at me as I attempt to wipe a tear from her face.

'And now you're telling me I won't get my wolf until you find your mate and fall in love with her?' She cries, 'Talk about a slap in the face, Magnus,'

'I'm sorry, Nina, I don't understand why the Moon Goddess would even take anything I say literally, anyway?'

'You have more muscle than brains. Do you know that?'

'What do you mean?'

'Your mother is from the Moonstone pack. She is a descendant of the Moon Goddess, which makes you a descendant also! So, of course, the Moon Goddess will take her descendants seriously! Ergh!' Nina stomps her feet and storms off.

I chase after her.

CHAPTER 34

'I'm sorry, that never crossed my mind,' I fall to my knees, 'I'm the biggest idiot ever to exist,' Nina stops running and turns to listen to me. 'We were the best of friends once. I thought the pack saw me as a big joke. I pushed you away and ignored you for years because of it. Then I made things even worse. I cursed you, and now you don't have a wolf. And you won't be able to sense your mate until I find mine. All I ever wanted was to protect you and keep you safe, but all I've done is cause you hurt and pain. I'm so sorry. Will you ever forgive me?' I ask.

Nina morbidly approaches me and falls to her knees in front of me. Our knees are touching. She takes my hands and holds them in hers. I can feel her hands trembling.

We gaze at each other with tear-filled eyes. Nina bursts into tears and wraps her arms around my neck. I hold her tight and cry into her soft brown hair.

'All those years, you say you ignored me. You never did. Every day we had breakfast and dinner together, you would stare at me with a longing in your eyes. When you climbed trees and swam through the lake with the others, you would always look to see if I had followed. When you saw me, your lips would curl into a smile, which you would quickly hide. The days I watched, and you couldn't see me. You were miserable and agitated towards the others. Throughout high school, every girl would try to get your attention, but you would still sit near me and watch me. Even Claire and May were always catching you staring at me. I could constantly sense your eyes on me as if you were caressing me with your own hands. As for the curse, you were only a child venting. If you had known it would become a curse, I know those words would have never left your lips. I forgive you, Magnus,' she says.

I squeeze her tighter and press my face further into her hair and neck.

'Thank you,' I whisper.

We part and wipe the tears from our faces.

'What do we do now?' I ask.

'The only thing left to do is make things right by finding your mate to break this curse,'

'We have to visit all the packs. Let's start with the Starlight pack east from here,'

We wait a couple of hours for the sun to rise.

Without warning, Nina grabs my arm, 'Wait...,'

'Skedaddle Dash, Skedaddle Dash, Skedaddle Dash.' Nina says.

My stomach churns as we flash one thousand metres east at a time until we reach Star Light territory. I instantly fall to the ground with severe nausea holding my stomach.

'Next time, please warn me to brace myself, Nina?'

'Don't be such a baby, Magnus. It's not that bad. I don't feel any motion sickness at all,'

'Maybe because you're the one casting the spell, you're immune to the effects?'

'Maybe karma is just getting you back for cursing me?' She smirks.

'You forget that when I cursed you to be wolfless, it cursed me by not being able to shift without immense pain.' I say sitting up.

Everything has stopped spinning. As soon as I stand, growls are heard around us. I pull Nina behind me to see five wolves circle us. Then, a wolf shifts back into its human form.

'You are trespassing in Starlight territory,' A male warns.

'I'm Magnus, the future Alpha of the Shadow Crest pack. I apologise for trespassing and the lack of notice of my arrival. I must meet every unmated she-wolf to find my mate. Please escort me to your Alpha,'

His eyes slightly fade. He is mind-linking his Alpha.

'This way,' he says. 'It will be quicker if you both shift,'

Nina and I give each other a worried look.

'Oh, but the weather is so… lovely that I think I'd like to walk?' She says it as a question rather than a statement.

She subtly shrugs her shoulders and whispers, 'What else am I to say? Sorry, I have no wolf, but that's okay. I'm a witch and can blink instead?'

'Okay… sure, I guess.' The man says, confused.

The wolves walk behind us as we are led to the packhouse. The rest of the wolves shift back into their human forms and enter the Packhouse after us.

'Beta Ryan, thank you for bringing Magnus to me. Fetch us some wine for our guests, will you?'

'Of course, Alpha Edward,' he bows and walks away.

'And who is this beautiful young she-wolf you have with you?' Alpha Edward asks me.

'This is Nina, she is the daughter of my pack's commander,'

'I see,' he smiles.

'Please take a seat, both of you.' He gestures his hands to the table. We take a chair and sit at the table. Nina sits beside me as we face Alpha Edward. Beta Ryan fills the glasses up with wine and hands one to Alpha Edward, then Nina and me.

'Beta Ryan tells me you are here to search for your mate?'

'Yes, Alpha Edward. I am,'

'Well, aren't you an eager Alpha to be wanting to find your mate so soon?' He chuckles.

299

'Very eager, Alpha Edward,'

'I see. Let's drink, and I'll have the she-wolves called up.'
He mind-links Ryan to ready the unmated she-wolves.

We finish our wine and follow Alpha Edward out the
door.

Two dozen she-wolves blush and twirl their hair as soon
as they see me approaching. I walk up to each one. My
wolf is calm, and I don't feel the pull from the mate bond
with them. I shake my head no at Alpha Edward. The girls
voice their disappointment that Magnus isn't their mate. A
pigeon flies over my head and lands on the stone
windowsill of the packhouse.

'Hmm, it's a messenger bird,' Alpha Edward says and
takes the paper scroll from the bird's leg.

He scrunches his eyebrows as he reads the note.

'You never told me rogues attacked your pack?'

'Oh, didn't I?' I say nervously.

'We are sending this letter out to all packs to inform
them that Shadow Crest was under attack through the
night by a pack of rogues who followed the orders from

Vanessa. Who you may all remember as Alpha Zenith's daughter from Shady Crest many years ago?

If anyone sees Magnus, please tell him we are okay and that we hope to see him and Nina home soon. Regards Alpha Ryker and the Luna, Astrid.'

'I'm sorry, Alpha Edward, when we were under attack, Nina was in great danger. So I had to leave Shadow Crest to keep her safe,'

'Well, now you can return since you know Shadow Crest is okay,' he smiles.

'It's not that easy, Alpha Edward. Nina will remain in danger until I find my mate. Until then, neither of us can return,'

'I don't understand how finding your mate will keep Nina safe?'

'It's complicated and information I cannot share without further endangering Nina. We thank you for your time and must make our way to the next pack. I'm sure it won't be long until you hear the rumours of why Nina is in danger. If you could reply to my parent's message and let them know I will return once I find my fated mate? We would appreciate it.'

Alpha Edward nods, and we take our leave.

Once we are out of sight, Nina grabs my arm, 'Skedaddle Dash,' she says, and we port halfway through the woods.

'We should set up camp for the night here?' She says as I vomit in the bushes.

'Sure,' I say before heaving again. Nina takes a bottle of water out of my bag and hands it to me.

'Thanks,'

Once my stomach is back in one place, I collect sticks and bundle them together.

'Inferno Flamo,' Nina says, igniting the fire.

'Are you ever going to warn me before you cast a spell?'

'Umm, probably not.' Nina smirks.

CHAPTER 35

We sit by the fire and keep warm. I lay on my back and looked up at the stars. Nina lies on her back next to me.

'I miss my Mum and Dad,' Nina says.

'I miss my family, too,' I reply.

'Would you believe I'm even missing May?'

'You, miss May? Never,' I smile.

'What if it's months or years until we ever see them again?'

'We have each other. You and me now against the world until I find my mate,' I sigh.

'Yeah,' Nina frowns and stands up. 'I'm going to go for a walk,'

'I'll come,'

'No, please stay. I need some time to myself. I won't go far. I promise,' she says with a sad expression.

'Oh, okay.'

I watch as she wanders further into the darkness of the woods. Why does she look so sad? I suppose she is going through a lot, having no wolf, a curse, and a witch hunt after her. I wish I could hold her, smell her mint and lavender hair, and tell her everything will be okay. If I could choose my fated mate, I would select Nina in a heartbeat.

Nina returns with red puffy eyes. She has been crying.

'Are you okay?'

'No, I'm not. I just want to go to sleep,' she says and lies on the other side of the fire away from me.

Why is she distancing herself from me? Did I say something that upset her?

I don't fall asleep until she is sound asleep.

When I wake up, it's the morning. I look over to where Nina slept. She isn't there.

'Nina, Nina!' I yell. I can't see her anywhere. 'Nina!' I frantically shout.

'What? Why are you yelling like that?' She says with hands full of berries. I race over to her, place my hands on her shoulder, and look her up and down.

'Are you okay? Where'd you go? I thought something bad happened to you?'

'You were still asleep, so I thought I'd pick us some berries for breakfast,'

I pull her in for a hug, squashing the berries she holds between us. She sighs. 'Well, there goes our breakfast,' she says.

'We can skip breakfast. Let's just get to the Midnight pack,'

'Fine... Skedaddle Dash, Skedaddle Dash.'

I keep my eyes closed longer than usual until we are no longer blinking. Then, after a minute, I slowly open my eyes and am relieved to have no nausea.

'That's more like it.' I smile.

We arrive near the Midnight Packhouse. I can see it further up the road. It's looking worse for wear and could do with fresh paint.

We walk towards the Packhouse. As I'm about to knock, I realise Nina, and I have been holding hands. When she realises too, she quickly lets go, and her smile fades. I want to ask her what is wrong. As I'm about to, the front door opens.

'I thought I could smell unfamiliar wolf scents,'

'Alpha Anslo, it's been a few years since I've seen you,' I say.

'Magnus, is that you? After I thought you couldn't grow any bigger here, you are, well, bigger,' he laughs. 'Come inside and join us for breakfast,'

'Breakfast is just what we need,' I smile.

We sit in the guest's seats at the table.

'Grab a plate and help yourselves,' Alpha Anslo says. 'Other than breakfast, what brings you to the Midnight pack?'

'I've been going to each pack hoping to find my mate,'

'I see. You are welcome to wander around and see if any of my pack members are lucky enough to be mated with you,'

'Thank You, Alpha Anslo.'

Nina and I walk through the Midnight pack territory with full stomachs. Nina drifts behind me. Every time I look at her, I can tell she is forcing a fake smile, but why?

'Stop staring at me already and find your mate, Magnus,' she says.

'Is something wrong, Nina?'

'No, why would anything be wrong?' She frowns.

'I just can't help but feel there is something you want to tell me?'

Nina hugs herself and looks down.

'That depends... is there something you want to tell me?' She says with hope in her voice.

I take a step closer to her, 'I-I um...'

'There he is,' a she-wolf yells.

Half a dozen she-wolves come running up to me. Nina backs away, and her hopeful smile disappears again.

They take my hands and pull me towards the houses as more she-wolves come out. Even though I am being dragged away, I turn my head to watch Nina walk away towards the Packhouse.

She doesn't want to come with me to meet the she-wolves. I don't understand why. You would think she would be keen for me to find my mate so I can break her curse once and for all. But I don't get her sometimes.

After meeting all the available she-wolves, I hadn't felt my mate bond with them. They were very disappointed that I wasn't their mate. I return to the packhouse.

'So, tell me, was any of the ladies your mate?' Alpha Anslo asks.

'No,' I sigh.

'Well, that's very unfortunate. I wish you luck in the next pack,'

'Thanks, we should get going,' I say and look over at Nina. She seems withdrawn. We leave the packhouse and enter the woods.

'So, which pack are we going to next?' She asks.

'Let's set up camp for the night. We can worry about the next pack in the morning.'

We silently collect sticks together and bundle them up.

'Inferno Flamo,' Nina says, lighting the fire.

She sits on the other side of the fire and avoids eye contact.

'Nina, I can't help but feel you have been distancing yourself from me? You have been avoiding me, and you didn't even want to help me find my mate today. I'm starting to think you don't want me to break the curse?'

She looks up at me wide-eyed, with her beautiful doe eyes. Her eyes well.

I scoot over to her.

'What's wrong? Please tell me?'

'I don't want to upset you or worsen the situation,'

'Nina, seeing you upset is upsetting me. The only time I am ever truly happy is when you are smiling and when we are together?'

'Really?'

'Yes, really.'

'It hurts when I see all the she-wolves swoon over you. I know you need to find your mate, but I care about you. I always wished as a child you would be my fated mate,' she sobs.

'You wished I was your mate?' I ask as my heart rate rapidly increases. A feeling of happiness washes over me at her words.

'Yes, it's stupid. I know,'

I cup her face in my hands, gaze down into her brown eyes, and suddenly realise that I don't just love Nina as my best friend, but that I'm deeply in love with Nina.

'Nina, I think we can go back home now,' I smile.

She gives me a look of confusion.

'But we haven't found your mate yet?'

'We don't need to find her. I have everything I ever dreamed of right in front of me,'

'Magnus, what are you saying?' She trembles in shock.

'Nina, it's you I love. It's you who I want to spend the rest of my life with, even if it means I never shift again and you never have your wolf. We don't need to have the mate bond to know we love each other. I don't need to feel electricity when we touch, but the warmth of your soft skin. Nina, I want to be with you. I love you,' I say.

'Magnus,' she sobs. 'I love you too,' she says as we gaze lovingly into each other's eyes.

We kiss with the utmost passion. A crack of lightning strikes a tree nearby, and thunder roars through the sky. Nina wraps her arms around my neck, and I wrap mine around her waist as the kiss intensifies.

Suddenly Nina flinches back and screams in pain as a bone snaps.

She is shifting. The curse is broken.

CHAPTER 36

More thunder and lightning flash through the sky above
us and turns into a wild storm raining down on us. As I
hold Nina in my lap, I feel the tingly static where we
touch. It feels amazing. Our eyes turn black. 'Mate,' we say
in unison.

Nina lets out another scream.

'Try not to fight it, Nina. It will hurt less if you let your
wolf take over,' I say, stroking my fingers through her
hair.

'It hurts,'

'I know, babe. I'm here, and I will help you through this.'

She nods and tries her best to relax. Black fur covers her
as she shifts into her wolf. My breath is taken away. Her

wolf is pure black with a white-shaped star on her forehead.

'Nina, your wolf is so beautiful. You even have a white star on your forehead. I've never seen anything like this,' I say, stroking her fur. She steps back, prances happily in wolf form, and then nudges into my shoulder.

'You want me to shift too?'

She nods her head.

'Well, if the curse is broken, I shouldn't feel any pain when I shift.'

I remove my clothes and focus my mind, closing my eyes for a moment. Then, I open them to find I have shifted straight away, pain-free, into my sizeable white wolf.

'This is amazing,' I think to her.

'I can hear you!' Nina replies.

'I can hear you too we can mind-link now!'

'We were fated mates all along. Can you believe that?' Nina cries.

'We were never cursed, Nina. On the contrary, we had been blessed with each other all along.'

We rub our furry faces all over each other affectionately.

314

'Let's run home,' I mind-link.

Nina runs ahead with super speed. I can only just keep up behind her. We run for hours through the night until we are exhausted. Then, we lie huddled together and stare up at the moon.

'Moon Goddess, thank you for blessing me with Nina as my mate,'

Nina nudges me and shifts back into her human form. I shift back, too.

'That was amazing. We can both shift now, and we are fated, mates!' Nina squeals and plonks herself happily in my lap. I nuzzle my face into her neck and inhale her Lavender and Mint scent.

'You smell so good,' I say.

Nina giggles as my nose tickles her neck.

'You smell like chocolate and freshly chopped wood,' she laughs.

'Really?'

'Yep,' she grins.

Without warning, my mouth crashes onto hers, and we share a passionate moment.

'Shall we skedaddle the rest of the way back home?' She asks.

'Yes, let's go,'

Embraced in my arms, she waves her wand around. 'Skedaddle Dash, Skedaddle Dash, Skedaddle Dash.'

We blink multiple times until we reach Shadow Crest, except we land in the water at Shadow Crest Lake.

We burst into laughter in the middle of the lake. It's still dark, but the sun will rise soon.

We kiss and wrap our arms around each other. Our teeth protrude through our moment of passion, and we run our elongated teeth across the nape of each other's neck. We ready ourselves to mark each other. My teeth sink into the nape of Nina's neck, and hers sink into my neck. A euphoric sense takes over us as we mark each other. We are officially mates. Nina is mine.

We lie on the grass as the sun rises, and we sleep as we wait for our clothes to dry. It's almost lunchtime when we wake.

Nina is smiling and flinches when she touches the mark on her neck.

'Tender?'

'Yeah, but that's expected,' she smiles.

'We better get dressed. I can't wait to announce that you are my mate.' I smile.

Holding hands, we giggle and laugh together as we walk through the town of Shadow Crest. Everyone stares and whispers. We arrive back home at the packhouse. Still holding hands, we enter together to see our families at the dining table about to have lunch.

'Magnus,' My parents yell excitedly.

'Nina!' Her parents shout happily.

Everyone runs over to us, including Zak, Josie, Flint, May, and Pipsqueak.

They come to a stop and look down at our hands, holding.

'Magnus, what is going on?' Astrid asks, confused.

'We broke the curse. I told Nina it is her I want, that I love her, and I want to be with her forever even if it means me never shifting and her never gaining her wolf. We don't need to have the mate bond to know we love each other. We kissed, and she shifted. I can shift without pain

317

as well. And you should all see her wolf! She is so beautiful,' I turn Nina towards me. 'Just like her human form.' I say and kiss her in front of everyone.

Everyone is crying tears of happiness. My Dad and Leon shake hands, and our mothers hug each other.

There is a commotion outside. I open the front door to see half the town yelling.

'What is the problem?' I ask.

'There she is, the witch!' Pack members yell, pointing at Nina behind me.

'This witch will soon be your Luna, so be careful what you say!'

'We will never accept a witch as our Luna, she doesn't even have a wolf!' Another person yells.

I smile at Nina to shift. She immediately morphs into her wolf, and everyone gasps at her unique and beautiful black wolf with the white star.

'Your Luna is one of us! She may be half-wolf- half-witch, but you will all love and respect her as I do! Anyone that upsets or aggravates my fated mate that the Moon

Goddess blessed me with and blessed you all with will suffer great consequences at the wave of her wand,'

'What consequences?' Someone asks.

'Nina has my blessing to turn anyone of you into a frog if you disrespect her,' I say.

Nina is trying not to laugh. She knows she can't turn anyone into a frog. Not yet anyway.

The crowd gasps and dissipates, worried Nina will turn them into frogs.

'I'll see you all at the ceremony announcing Nina and me as your official Luna and Alpha.' I say, waving.

***

One week later.

Nina and I walk hand in hand into the ceremony hall.

My parents await us on the stage. We walk up together and stand facing my parents.

'It is with great honour I hand over my status as Alpha to my first-born child, Magnus,' Ryker says.

'And it is with great honour I hand over my status as Luna to my son's fated mate, Nina.' Astrid smiles.

'With that said, I announce your new Luna, Nina, and your new Alpha, Magnus,' Ryker says.

The hall erupts with cheers.

I stand behind Nina, wrap my arms around her, and place a kiss on her head. She leans back against my chest and looks up at me, smiling.

'You can let me go now,' she blushes.

'Nina, I'll never let you go.'

ABOUT THE AUTHOR

Jazz Ford is a wife and mother of three children. She lives in Geelong, Victoria, Australia. Jazz is a former Personal Care Attendant with a background in nursing homes and in-home care. She loves writing full-time from home. In her spare time, she enjoys photography, graphic design with photoshop, and spending time with her husband and children. Jazz Ford's other works are 'The Alpha King's Mate', 'Alpha Maximus: The Last Lycan', 'The CEO' and many more. You can find Jazz on TikTok, Facebook and Instagram.

Made in United States
North Haven, CT
11 October 2022

25299448R00200